Healy stood amid the [...] *let grief wash over him* [...]

He lifted a maroon polo shirt and imagined how Tom's broad shoulders must have filled it out. His fists knotted around the coarse cotton fabric. *Lord, why? Why'd You bring me all this way, only to let me find out my best friend is dead?*

Pastor Henke appeared at the door, carrying a plastic tote containing cleaning supplies. "Valerie thought you might want to start getting the place habitable."

Healy shook off his grief. "Thanks. Good idea."

While they cleaned and sorted, the pastor told Healy a little more about the Paige family and their association with Zion. "Connor's an elder, and Ellen was leading a ladies' Bible study until she passed the baton to Bonnie Trapp last spring."

"And Valerie?" Healy's question was muffled by the stack of musty-smelling beige towels he carried to the bathroom.

"As a matter of fact, she just agreed to be our new prayer-chain coordinator." Pastor Henke clucked his tongue. "A worthy vocation, but such a waste when she could be doing so much more."

Healy's heart clenched with concern for his friend's widow. The moment he first laid eyes on her, he'd felt strong protective impulses rising from deep within his bones. He'd do anything, dare anything, if he could ease her sorrow and erase the fear that lurked behind those shimmering gray eyes.

MYRA JOHNSON has roots that go deep into Texas soil, but she's proud to be a new Oklahoman. Myra and her husband have two married daughters and five grandchildren. Empty nesters now, they share their home with two loveable dogs and a snobby parakeet. *Autumn Rains*, Myra's first novel for Heartsong Presents, won the 2005 RWA Golden Heart for Best Inspirational Romance Manuscript.

Autumn Rains

Myra Johnson

Heartsong Presents

For my terrific brother-in-law, Pastor James Hinkhouse, whose experience meeting a real-life "Healy Ferguson" inspired this story, and for my Golden Heart "forever friends," Janet Dean, Julie Lessman, and Tina Russo.

A note from the Author:
I love to hear from my readers! You may correspond with me by writing:

Myra Johnson
Author Relations
PO Box 721
Uhrichsville, OH 44683

ISBN 978-1-60260-626-5

AUTUMN RAINS

Our mission is to publish and distribute inspirational products offering exceptional value and biblical encouragement to the masses.

PRINTED IN THE U.S.A.

one

The Greyhound bus lurched to a stop in a swirling cloud of diesel fumes. Healy Ferguson heaved his long legs into the aisle and slung his ragged duffel bag over his shoulder. When he stepped off the bus, the heat slammed into him with the force of a 250-pound linebacker.

"Welcome to St. Louis," he muttered. Still, he hadn't seen so much sunshine in the past sixteen years, and it felt good. Real good.

Inside the ultramodern Gateway Transportation Center, smells from the food court set his stomach rumbling. He plunged his hand into his jeans pocket and fished out his cash. Nine dollars and seventy-three cents. At least he still had another twenty stashed between the pages of the Bible tucked away in his duffel bag.

Pathetic. He might have to choose between a late lunch and taxi fare to Tom's place.

If his best friend even lived in St. Louis anymore.

If, after all this time, Tom still thought of him as a friend.

Healy collapsed onto the nearest empty seat. *Lord, why did I ever come here? Why did I think Tommy would want to see me again?*

He hadn't heard from his friend in over four years. Maybe Tom's silence was his way of separating himself from a guy he should have written off as a loser from day one. Yeah, Ol' Tom must have finally come to his senses.

Awash in discouragement, Healy raked a hand across his forehead. He'd somehow managed to get stuck in a strange city with practically no money and no idea where to turn.

Except to You, Lord, except to You.

His stomach growled again. The bag of chips he'd picked up at the last stop had long since worn off, and the aroma of hamburgers on the grill enticed him like the fabled siren's song. But several other passengers swarmed the counters, and the wait looked to be a long one. He recalled passing some fast-food joints as they drove in, and after sitting so long, he could use a good walk.

But first a stop in the men's room. Entering a stall, he looped his duffel bag strap over the corner of the door, but before he'd even turned around, a hand snuck over the top and yanked the bag up and over.

"Hey, you!" Healy burst from the stall, too late to nab the thief. A guy with spiked hair and a gold stud in his lip shot Healy a smirk before disappearing through the restroom door. By the time Healy made it to the corridor, the creep was long gone.

Angry and out of breath, Healy collapsed against the wall. All his worldly possessions were in that duffel bag—*now what?* The idea of approaching a security guard made his stomach twist, but what choice did he have? Not that he expected he'd ever see his stuff again.

But Tom's Bible. . .he'd do anything to get that back. Spotting a uniformed cop patrolling the terminal, he caught up with him and tapped his arm. "Excuse me, sir. I've just been robbed."

The cop proved nice enough, taking Healy's report without belaboring his ignorance about restroom security. He explained they'd been on the alert for this guy for a couple of weeks now. "You got a phone number where I can reach you?"

"Uh, nope. Just got into town. Can I call you?"

The officer handed him a business card. "Don't get your hopes up, okay? And watch yourself. This is a big city."

As Healy thanked the man, a growl from the depths of his belly reminded him he still needed food. Except most of his cash had just disappeared along with the contents of his duffel bag. *Lord, I'm trusting in Your infinite provision.*

He felt in his pocket to make sure the rest of his money was safe and then found his way to the exit and out onto the street.

A few minutes later, the cashier at a hole-in-the-wall hamburger joint handed him his order in a greasy white bag. He took a seat at a sticky table and unwrapped his ninety-nine-cent burger. As he bit into the flattened sandwich, he felt like yelling, "Where's the beef?" They served better burgers where he came from, but no way did he wish to be there. Never again.

He popped the last french fry into his mouth and washed it down with a swig of watery cola. On the way to the restroom he stopped in the narrow hallway beside a payphone. A gigantic telephone book with soiled, ripped pages hung from a chain beneath the narrow shelf. He stared at the phone for long seconds. "Can't hurt to try, long as I'm here."

Balancing the book on his forearm, he paged through the residential section under *B*. He found a long list of Bishops, including several Toms, Thomases, and just plain *T*'s, but none of the street addresses matched what he remembered. He pictured the countless envelopes he'd addressed to 2418 Ashton Brook Lane, St. Louis, Missouri. Tom could have moved, and if Healy's letters weren't getting forwarded, maybe Tom came to believe Healy had broken off the friendship.

He frowned. He'd finish off his remaining coins long before he tried all those phone numbers. But Tom was worth the risk, whatever the cost.

Okay, better get started. He inserted some change and punched in a number. Two rings, three, four.

"Hi, y'all," chirped a recorded greeting—a woman's voice but heavy on the Southern drawl. "This is Tom and Amy's voice mail. Leave a message at the—"

Healy hung up. Unless Tom had remarried, his wife and college sweetheart was from Massachusetts and her name wasn't Amy. Besides, when Tom wrote several years ago, telling Healy all about his new bride, he sounded forever-after, head-over-heels in love.

He tried the next number. A teenager rudely told Healy he'd never heard of a Thomas Charles Bishop formerly of Gloucester, Massachusetts, and where in the—Healy winced at the curse—was Gloucester anyway?

He had enough change to make one more call. Maybe the restaurant Tom owned? He remembered it was Italian but couldn't recall the exact name. Too much time has passed since Tom's last letter. Too much Healy didn't want to remember. In shutting out the bad memories, he'd blurred a few important things as well.

"Lord, help me here. If I'm not supposed to find Tom, why'd You let me get on the bus to St. Louis in the first place?"

"Hey, buddy, you gonna make a call or not?"

He turned to face a short, tough-looking guy with a red-eyed rattlesnake tattoo glaring from his bicep. Healy edged away from the phone, his hands lifted in surrender. "Sorry. It's all yours."

He trudged out of the restaurant, met once again by intense heat rising off the shimmering sidewalk. With no goal in mind, he walked the sizzling streets until he found himself at the Mississippi River. Sweat ran in rivulets down his torso. He never realized Missouri could get this hot and humid.

And all this way for nothing. If only he could recall more details. Tom's wife had family in the area, Healy knew that much, but he couldn't remember any names, much less what city they lived in.

And Tom's letters were long gone, stolen by another tattooed tough guy, a newbie at the rooming house who didn't share Healy's taste in Christian music. Healy could only watch helplessly as the last ties to his only friend on earth took a nosedive into a flaming trash can.

And now he didn't even have the Bible, the one Tom gave him the last time he visited.

"I'm off to that little college in Boston I told you about," Tom had told him. "Might not get back to Michigan any time soon, so I wanted you to have this Bible to remember me by. Hang on to it, Gus." Tom always called him by the nickname—short for Ferguson—he'd bestowed when they first met on the high school football team. "This book holds the words of life."

Words of life that had sustained Healy through a torturous decade and a half. Now he wanted to find and personally thank the man who'd shared faith and hope with him, who had, at least a long time ago, believed in Healy Ferguson when others turned their backs.

The late afternoon sun reflecting off the murky Mississippi told him he'd soon need to make plans for the night. Maybe he could curl up in one of the bus station seats until morning, then decide how to pay for a ticket back to. . .

No, there'd be no going back. How did the worn-out cliché go? *Today is the first day of the rest of your life.* He'd dreamed of a new start. Tom or no Tom, with God's help maybe St. Louis could be just that.

He made it back to the transportation center shortly before sunset, but his long, aimless walk had left him sweaty, parched, and hungry again. He could wash up in the restroom, then break out his remaining cash and buy himself a little supper. Possibly his last meal if he didn't figure out something quick.

❧

A crash and a shout of pain shattered the afternoon stillness. The fountain pen flew from Valerie Bishop's hand, sending a spray of ink across the journal page. She fought to drag her thoughts away from the bittersweet memories she'd been reliving. *The security system—had someone—*

"Mrs. Bishop, are you up there? I need help."

Her head cleared instantly. "Mr. Garcia!"

She hurried downstairs, gasping for breath by the time she reached the living room. The gray-haired handyman lay in a heap next to his toppled ladder on the paint-spattered drop cloth.

Valerie rushed over to kneel beside him. "What happened? Are you hurt?"

He clutched his thigh, grimacing. "My leg. I think it's broken."

"Don't move. I'll call 911." She raced to the kitchen phone and placed the call, then returned and retrieved a pillow from beneath the plastic tarp covering the sofa. Gently she placed it under Mr. Garcia's head. "An ambulance is on the way. Does it hurt much?"

"Only when I breathe." He offered a weak smile. "My own fault, trying to paint twelve-foot walls with a six-foot ladder. Too stubborn to go out to the truck for the longer one." He shifted his weight and let out a groan.

"Careful, you could be hurt worse than you think." Valerie patted his arm as her glance took in the high walls, where a wide strip of mottled green near the ceiling contrasted with the fresh coat of eggshell white.

"Doc ain't gonna be happy about this," Mr. Garcia said. "I promised him I'd wrap things up by the end of the month."

"You let me worry about my brother," Valerie stated with an encouraging smile. Connor Paige and his wife, Ellen, had spent the last few years renovating the historic two-story Victorian. They'd hoped to have at least the lower floor completed in time for Connor's Fourth of July staff party, less than two weeks away.

"Aunt Val?" came a tentative voice from the top of the stairs. "I heard a bad noise."

"Down here, Annie." Valerie straightened, then strode to the hallway, ignoring the pull in her lower back. Honestly, some days she felt more like sixty than thirty. She rested a hand on the banister and looked up at her sleepy-eyed niece, whose flaxen ringlets lay matted against her damp brow. Except for Annie's natural curls, Valerie could have been looking at herself at age four.

As Annie trudged downstairs, dragging a stuffed rabbit by one ear, Valerie heard the squeal of brakes. Red and blue strobe lights sliced through the curtains. Once again, Valerie fought to still her racing heart and focus on the task at hand.

"Are those the doctor people? What happened?" Hugging her rabbit with one arm, the little girl gripped the hem of Valerie's sundress.

"Mr. Garcia fell from his ladder." As Valerie entered the alarm code on the keypad, she tried not to dwell on the fact that one light blinked steadily, indicating an open window in the living room, left ajar for ventilating the paint fumes.

Two paramedics entered. She directed them through the French doors. "Careful, there's wet paint."

Within seconds, three of the neighbors appeared in the entryway. Maggie Jensen, balancing a plump, red-haired toddler on her hip, spoke first. "We saw the ambulance drive up. Is everything okay?"

"Mr. Garcia took a bad fall." Valerie rubbed her arms and glanced toward the living room.

Jean Franklin, wearing tennis togs, pulled a stretch-terry sweatband off her short gray curls. "That's awful. Is he hurt very badly?"

"It's a broken leg, I think."

"And how are *you*?" Maggie placed her free arm around Valerie's shoulder.

She gave a wry grin and reached across to tousle little Steven's flaming locks. "A little shook up, but I'll be fine."

Cliff Reyna, the third neighbor, shrugged. "I'll get out of your way then, but you know where to find me if you need anything." He nodded toward his bungalow across the street.

Valerie smiled her gratitude. "I know, and I appreciate it more than I can say."

After the paramedics transferred Mr. Garcia to the ambulance and drove away, Valerie closed the door against the stifling heat. Thank goodness Connor's first remodeling priority had been installing central air conditioning. She expelled a tired sigh, then twisted the deadbolt and reset the alarm.

"Mr. Garcia didn't clean up his mess." Annie pointed to the cream-colored sludge oozing from the overturned paint tray.

Paint smells filled Valerie's nostrils. "Guess I'd better find someone who can finish the job."

Two hours later, Valerie hadn't yet lined up another painter. She shoved the phonebook across the kitchen table.

A key in the lock announced Ellen Paige's arrival home from teaching summer English classes at East Central College. After disabling the alarm, she dropped her shoulder bag on the table next to the phonebook. She dropped a quick kiss on Annie's head and collapsed into the nearest chair.

Valerie saw the fatigue in her sister-in-law's eyes. Probably the heat—it had been affecting them all. She walked to the refrigerator. "You look like you could use a cold drink."

"Sounds wonderful. Thanks." Glancing out the window, Ellen nodded toward the painter's truck parked in the driveway. "Mr. Garcia still at it?"

"Afraid not." Valerie returned with two glasses of ice water. She fortified herself with a long swallow, then explained about the accident.

"Poor man." Ellen furrowed her brow. "I hope he'll be okay."

"I'll call later and check on him. Maybe we could send over a meal." She poked at the ice cubes in her water glass. "I never thought to call anyone about picking up his truck and equipment. Maybe Mrs. Garcia can have someone come by."

"Mommy, you should have seed the doctor people," Annie said. "The amb'lance made a lot of noise. Can I have a cookie?"

"Too close to supper, sweetheart." Ellen coiled one of the tot's blond curls around her finger. "Any ideas where we could find someone to finish the painting, Val?"

"Everyone I've tried is already locked into other jobs, most of them for the rest of the summer." She pried open a bobby pin with her teeth and tucked a loose strand of hair into her topknot.

"Well, that fries it." Softening her expression, Ellen continued, "Honestly, Val, none of this work would be getting done if you weren't here to oversee things. Household manager, nanny, best friend—" She leaned across the table and gave Valerie a grateful hug. "You're the best sister-in-law ever."

"The feeling's mutual." She couldn't bring herself to imagine where she'd be without the generosity of her brother and his wife. Probably in a mental hospital somewhere. . .or worse. She refused to impose on her widowed mother, already overburdened with the care of Valerie's aging grandparents.

Ellen drained her glass. "So what are we going to do? Connor sure can't finish the painting himself, not with putting in ten-hour days seeing patients."

The image of her tall, sandy-haired brother holding a paintbrush made Valerie laugh. "Imagine how long it would take that perfectionist to paint one wall, much less an entire room!"

Ellen chortled. "Right. Connor better stick with plastic surgery, where his perfectionism is truly an asset."

The kitchen door whisked open, and Connor Paige breezed in. He kicked the door shut and tossed his car keys on the table. "You two talking about me behind my back again?"

"Honey, you're home early." Ellen self-consciously tugged at her ash brown curls as she greeted her husband with a kiss.

"Mmm, love you, too, babe." He drew her into his arms. "My last surgery of the day was canceled. The lady decided she liked her nose the way it was."

"Her loss, my gain." Ellen's voice became husky, and she melted into his embrace. "I get to rub noses with the handsomest guy in the world."

Valerie caught Annie's enraptured gaze and smiled to herself, drawing her own vicarious pleasure from seeing Connor and Ellen so much in love.

With a downward glance, she clenched her left fist and felt the pressure of her gold wedding band between her fingers.

Oh, Tom, I miss you so.

two

"Hey, hey you." A rough hand jostled Healy awake. "This ain't no hotel, ya know."

Pain shot through his neck as he tried to straighten from his slouched position. "Sorry." He rubbed his eyes and attempted to focus on the wiry, balding man standing over him.

"You been here all night," the man said, leaning on a broom handle. "I know, because I'm the janitor, and so have I." He dragged a sweat-stained handkerchief across his forehead and sank onto the seat beside Healy. "I'd'a had security kick you outta here a long time ago, except you look to be an honest guy who's temporarily down on his luck."

"Yeah, you could say that. Everything I own was stolen in the men's room yesterday."

"Bummer. Security's usually pretty tight here, but I heard they'd had a few problems lately. Wish I could help, but workin' in bus stations for nigh on thirty years, I learned real quick not to keep much cash on me."

"Thanks anyway. It's my own fault for being careless." Healy ran stiff fingers through his tangled hair. His mouth tasted like damp cardboard.

The janitor reached for a discarded section of newspaper and smoothed out the wrinkles. "This yours?"

"Naw, picked it up off the floor yesterday." He reached for the paper, folded open to a half-page advertisement for area churches. Last night, as he'd weighed his sadly limited options, he'd decided the best thing to do would be to seek assistance from a church, and one ad had snagged his attention. A white-haired, bespectacled pastor smiled warmly from an inch-tall grainy photo, bringing to mind

Healy's boyhood Sunday school teacher. And the name of the suburb—Aileen—had a familiar ring. He wondered if Tom had mentioned it before in his letters.

"You know that place?" Healy pointed to the ad. "The preacher looks like a nice guy."

The janitor took a closer look. "Aileen's down the road a fair piece. Quiet, country-like. Lots of fancy old homes, good place to raise kids."

Healy looked away, an ache tightening his throat. Aileen didn't sound much like a town where he'd fit in. And kids? Those came with a wife, a job, and stability.

Fat chance.

Still. . . *Aileen*. The name rolled around in his mind like a soothing melody. He glanced sideways at the janitor. "How far you say it is?"

"Maybe forty miles." He pointed over his shoulder. "Take I-44 past Gray Summit, then over toward Villa Ridge."

The highway and town names meant nothing to Healy, but he thanked the janitor and stood wearily. The food court had begun gearing up for breakfast, and the smells of sizzling bacon and brewing coffee pushed Healy's gnawing hunger into overdrive. A wave of dizziness made him stagger.

"Steady, there." The janitor grasped his arm. "When'd you eat last?"

"Yesterday, sometime." He'd spent the last of his money on a package of cheese crackers from a snack machine.

The janitor pulled his wallet from a pocket inside his coveralls. "My shift ends in twenty minutes anyway, so I'll give you what little I have. Buy yourself some breakfast."

Healy tried to shove the money away. "How will I pay you back?"

"Just do a good turn for somebody else you meet along the way." The janitor touched a finger to his forehead and returned to his cleaning cart.

Healy spent about five seconds offering up a prayer of

heartfelt thanks to his heavenly Provider, then stepped up to the counter and ordered coffee and pancakes. When he finished eating, he returned to the clerk and asked if he could purchase a tall cup of ice.

"And can you tell me how to get from here to Interstate 44?"

&

In the relative coolness of the June morning—the temperature just creeping into the eighties—Valerie sat in a wicker porch rocker and watched Annie play on her multicolored swing set. Two tall oaks and an ancient elm shaded the backyard; purple and fuchsia petunias cascaded from planters on the porch rail. The six-foot cedar fence and padlocked gates offered a semblance of security.

A sultry breeze toyed with a strand of Valerie's hair as she lifted the cordless phone from her lap. Reading from Mr. Garcia's business card, she dialed his home number. His wife put him on the line.

"Mrs. Bishop, so kind of you to call."

"I tried to phone last night, but you were probably still at the hospital. How are you?"

"Leg's gonna be fine, but I'll be staying off ladders for a while." Mr. Garcia chuckled, then his tone grew serious. "I'm real sorry to leave Doc Paige in a bind."

"It's okay, really. And Connor said to let him know if his hospital connections can be of any help."

"Thanks, I appreciate that."

The porch boards creaked under the rungs of Valerie's chair. "Any chance you know of someone who might fill in for you?"

"I can give you a couple names. . .but summer's a busy time."

"So I've discovered. I've already tried everyone in the Yellow Pages."

Mr. Garcia apologized again.

"Please, it's not your fault. We'll figure something out." She smirked. "At worst, we'll start a new Fourth of July tradition. We'll pass out T-shirts and coveralls, and Connor can make his get-together a painting party."

"Now there's a plan," Mr. Garcia said with a laugh. He told Valerie his wife and a friend would come by later for his truck and equipment.

She said good-bye and laid the phone on a glass-topped wicker side table.

"Come swing me, Aunt Val," Annie called. "Make me go high."

"Be right there." Valerie slipped her bare feet into the sandals she'd pushed aside.

The sun's glare reminded her of the latest weather report: heat and drought with no immediate end in sight. Valerie didn't miss the long winters and deep snows of Massachusetts, but this summer threatened to do her in. Thank goodness they weren't on mandatory water rationing, because the sprinkler system was the only thing keeping the lawn and garden plants alive.

She reached down to refasten a yellow barrette holding Annie's riot of curls off her damp face, then gave the swing a gentle push.

Annie giggled. "Higher, higher!"

Valerie tickled Annie's ribs on the next pass. "Any higher and you'll fly right over the roof."

The back door slammed, and Valerie looked up to see Ellen striding toward them.

"Hey, squirrel." Ellen waited for the swing to slow and then lifted Annie out. "How about a good-bye kiss before Mommy heads off to work?" As she planted her lips on the girl's head, she wrinkled her nose in disgust. "Sweaty, sweaty, sweaty. Phee-ewww!"

Annie squirmed away. "Oh, silly mommy!"

With a pat on the bottom, Ellen sent Annie off to play, then draped an arm around Valerie's shoulder. "After we get the little stinker into bed tonight, Connor and I have something important to talk to you about."

Concern prickled the back of Valerie's neck. Leave it to Ellen to drop a bomb like that and then make her wait all day for the rest of the story. She could certainly guess what the "something important" might be. A married couple deserved privacy, and Valerie lived in dread of the day Connor and Ellen would tell her she needed to pull herself together once and for all, move out, and live her own life.

And she simply wasn't ready.

❧

If not for the problem of finding another painter, Valerie might have spent the entire day brooding over Ellen's cryptic words.

Father, she prayed, taking the cordless phone from its cradle in the kitchen nook, *I know it's long past time for me to be living independently again—but the very thought terrifies me. Have I taken Connor and Ellen too much for granted?*

Exhaling through tight lips, she pressed the numbers for the pastor's office at Zion Community Church. "Good morning, Pastor. It's Valerie Bishop."

"Hello, my dear, how are you on this sweltering summer day?"

The image of the jolly, white-haired man smiling into the telephone cheered her immediately. With his scholarly mannerisms and cultured accent, he reminded her of an eccentric old Anglican vicar. She often wondered how he'd ended up shepherding their small-town congregation in Aileen, but the folks at Zion adored him.

Valerie peeked into the den to check on Annie, then carried the phone back to the kitchen. "I'm in a bit of a quandary, and I'm hoping you can help. You've probably heard about Phil Garcia's accident." She lowered herself gently into a chair.

Pastor Henke laughed. The painter's wife also happened to be the church librarian. "Harriet has made sure everybody in the office knows, and the ladder gets higher and the leg cast bigger every time she tells the story."

"I feel horrible for him." She sighed. "The problem is, we haven't found anyone else to finish the renovations, and I thought you might know of someone. Perhaps an Eagle Scout looking for a project, or maybe a bored retired person who'd like a little extra income."

"Let me put my thinking cap on. Can I get back to you?"

"Of course." She closed her eyes. "You know where to find me."

"Valerie," Pastor Henke began.

She winced at his cajoling tone. "Please, Pastor, don't start on me again."

"All right, but this has gone on quite long enough, my dear, and I absolutely refuse to give up on you."

As she said good-bye, Valerie couldn't help but smile. The pastor had been offering his tender counsel ever since she moved to Aileen four years ago to live with her brother. The panic attacks had started even before Valerie was released from the hospital after the accident. The doctors called it *post-traumatic stress disorder*. Valerie only knew that on the night Tom died, she lost not only all semblance of security but all her hopes for the family she'd dreamed of creating with the love of her life.

Thank You again, Father, for Connor and Ellen. Their invitation to share their home had been the best thing she could have hoped for at the lowest point in her life.

With a grateful sigh, she retrieved the glass of iced tea she'd left by the phone cradle and pressed its coolness to her cheek.

❧

Hot. Healy couldn't remember when he'd ever been so hot. When he began his trek shortly before eight that morning, a bank thermometer had read eighty-six degrees. Eighty-six that early in the day? What had he gotten himself into? Summer in Michigan would have seemed downright balmy in comparison.

But Michigan held nothing for him now. It felt like a whole other lifetime, one he'd just as soon forget.

Long after he'd finished off his melted ice and refilled his cup several times from gas-station water hoses, a robust trucker pulled over and offered Healy a ride.

"How far you headed, son?" The man shot him a toothy smile.

"Aileen." Healy basked in the cool of the air conditioner wafting through the open cab door. He pulled the rolled section of newspaper from his back pocket and pointed to the listing for Zion Community Church. "I'm going there."

"Aileen, huh? I can get you as far as Gray Summit. That's where I dump my load. Aileen's maybe six or seven miles off the highway from there."

"Close enough." Healy grinned his thanks and climbed into the cab.

The half-hour ride gave him a chance to rest his weary legs and quench his thirst with the frosty lemon-lime soda the trucker offered him from his cooler. The trucker wheeled the big rig into the loading area behind a warehouse. "End of the line for me, son. Hope you can find another ride for the rest of the way."

"God bless you for your kindness."

The driver pointed him in the direction of Aileen, and Healy resumed his sweltering trek.

Following the signs, he trudged along a winding two-lane road. He passed country estates, farms, and rolling meadows where horses, sheep, and small herds of cattle grazed. The withered grass and shrinking ponds gave evidence of the early summer heat wave.

Around the next bend, he caught sight of the Aileen city limit sign. POPULATION 2,376. He groaned. How many job opportunities could there be in a town this small?

But he couldn't shake the sense that God had led him here, led him to Aileen and the kind-faced pastor of Zion Community Church.

When he reached the town square, he spotted the church directly across the green. Stained-glass windows framed the double doors of the white clapboard building. A tall bell tower with a gold cross on top cut a bright slash across the cloudless sky. A sign indicated the pastor's office could be found at the rear of the building. Healy followed a narrow sidewalk between neatly manicured flowerbeds and came upon a small outbuilding behind the church. He knocked and entered uncertainly.

"Come in and close the door," came a cheery voice, "before you let all the cool air out."

Seeing the round-faced man behind the cluttered desk, Healy recognized him as the pastor in the newspaper photo. "Excuse me, sir, I—"

The pastor's mouth dropped open. His eyes widened. Healy could only imagine what he must look like, barging in off the street in a sweat-soaked T-shirt and filthy jeans. Not to mention he needed a shave, and his last haircut wasn't exactly *GQ* material.

Face it. You look like what you are, an ex-con. You were wrong to come here. Aileen is definitely not your kind of town.

"I, uh. . .sorry to bother you." He lowered his head and started out the door.

"Don't go." The pastor scurried around the desk. "Here, have a seat." He took Healy by the arm and guided him toward an ancient sofa upholstered in green corduroy. "Please forgive my rudeness. I was expecting someone else, that's all."

He closed the door and stood before Healy. "Now, young man, you look as if you're in need of some help. Please tell me what I can do."

Healy gulped. Since he'd arrived in St. Louis yesterday, three perfect strangers had befriended him. He didn't know what to do with such undeserved kindness. He braced his arms on his thighs and sighed.

The short, plump pastor plopped down beside him. "My,

that's some scar." He pointed to the six-inch strip of dimpled white flesh on Healy's left forearm. "May I ask how it happened?"

Healy pressed his lips together, his answer barely audible. "Knife fight."

The pastor sat back and folded his hands. "Sounds like you have quite a story to tell."

three

Valerie sat in Connor's paneled study overlooking the sunny front lawn. One hand resting on a computer mouse, she scrolled down a Web page and selected two boxes of shredded wheat to add to her online grocery order.

"What else, Miss Annie?" she asked the squirming girl in her lap.

"Cookies."

"You and your cookies." Valerie tickled Annie's tummy until the little girl doubled over in giggles. She selected another item from a dropdown menu. "Okay, what kind? Oatmeal? Chocolate chip?"

Annie pointed to a picture of peanut butter sandwich cookies. "Those kinds."

Valerie moved the cursor and clicked. "Your wish is my command. Hop down now, and let me finish. Then we'll have time for one more game before Mommy and Daddy get home."

"Yay! I'll go pick one." Spiraled pigtails jiggling, Annie dashed out of the study.

Valerie released an envious groan at the little girl's bubbling energy. Turning to the computer screen, she selected the Submit Order button. While she waited for the confirmation message, she wondered again what Ellen and Connor planned to tell her tonight.

After dinner, she had to suppress her anxiety awhile longer as she washed up the dishes and Ellen got Annie into the tub for a bubble bath. Two bedtime stories later, followed by Annie's nightly prayer in which she blessed everyone including the postman, the church custodian, and the Jensens' three-legged dog, Connor and Ellen finally settled their little girl into bed. Valerie followed their kisses and hugs with several of her own, and the three adults tiptoed downstairs to the quiet kitchen.

"Con, honey, a tall glass of cold milk would sure taste good right now." Ellen set out some glasses. "Some for you, Val?"

"Sure. I'll break out the graham crackers."

"Three tall white ones, coming up." Connor hefted the milk jug from the refrigerator.

"All right, you two, what's going on?" Valerie's voice rang with forced brightness as she joined her brother and sister-in-law at the table. Dread tightened its grip on her heart, and she hoped they didn't notice her trembling hand as she passed around the box of grahams.

Connor and Ellen exchanged looks.

"You should tell her, Con," Ellen said.

"I'm surprised you didn't let it slip already." Dodging Ellen's playful slap, Connor glanced at Valerie. "Okay, here's the deal, sis. I, uh, we're. . ." His jaw clenched.

Dry graham cracker crumbs lodged in Valerie's throat. She sipped her milk and swallowed hard. "Just say it, Connor. You're scaring me."

He laughed nervously. "It's just that we're hoping you'll be as happy about this as we are. Ellen and I—we're going to have another baby."

"Oh. Oh, my goodness. That's wonderful!" The knot of anxiety swelled into a teary explosion of joy. She almost tipped over her milk glass in the rush to embrace her brother and his wife. "How long have you known?"

Ellen handed her a napkin to dry her eyes. "I was starting to get suspicious, so we did a pregnancy test last night. According to my calculations, the baby's due in early February—right around Annie's birthday." She held Valerie at arm's length, her brows furrowed. "Are you okay with this? I mean, *really*?"

"Why wouldn't I be?" Valerie hugged her sister-in-law again. "I know how much you've been wanting another child. And Annie will be thrilled to have a new baby brother or sister."

Connor wrapped his arm around her waist. "You've been so great with Annie, and then taking charge of the renovations and all." He glanced up at her with concern. "The thing is, we don't want the baby to be an additional burden."

Valerie stepped back, her fears crashing in again. "Connor, don't you realize that being a nanny to your children is the best thing that could ever happen to me?" *Or second-best.* She clamped down on the fresh surge of regret.

Connor grinned. "We were hoping you'd still feel that way."

Relief flooded her—they weren't sending her on her way after all!

But as she returned to her seat, Valerie's heart constricted with a new concern. "Ellen, the paint fumes. You shouldn't even be in this house."

"Connor and I run the air purifier in our bedroom, and we use those high-efficiency filters in the AC." She cast Valerie a look of loving accusation. "The fumes aren't good for you, either. When we find another painter, I wish you and Annie would. . .could go out. . ." She let her words trail off with a helpless shrug.

"Annie and I are fine. We spend most mornings playing in the backyard. When it gets too hot, we stay in the den with the door closed. And Mr. Garcia was always good about cracking a window for ventilation." Although she never wasted any time closing and locking the windows after he finished for the day.

"You know what Ellen's trying to say, Val," Connor said in a low voice, "and it's not about paint fumes."

She couldn't meet his eyes. "I know."

Later, alone in her bedroom, she permitted her full range of emotions to surface. In spite of the joy flooding her at the thought of a precious new niece or nephew, her heart threatened to break in two. "Oh, dear Lord, when will You take away the pain? When will You fill up this horrible, aching emptiness? Will I ever feel whole again?"

She stared at the ink-stained journal entry she'd been writing in yesterday when Mr. Garcia fell. Words leaped out at her. *My precious one. . .never forget you. . .in my heart to stay.*

She moved the book aside and pulled a crisp sheet of stationery from the drawer. When she reached for her Bible, it fell open easily to one of her favorite psalms, number 139, and she copied the verses with flowing script:

> *For you created my inmost being;*
> *you knit me together in my*
> *mother's womb. . . .*
> *My frame was not hidden from you*
> *when I was made in the*
> *secret place. . . .*
> *All the days ordained for me were*
> *written in your book*
> *before one of them came to be.*

When the ink dried, she carefully folded the paper in thirds and slid it into an envelope. Across the front, she wrote:

> *Dearest Connor and Ellen,*
> *May the Lord continue to bless your very special family. Thank you for letting me be a part of it.*
>
> > *Valerie*

She tiptoed into the darkened master bedroom and turned on the bedside lamp. Laying the envelope atop Ellen's Bible on the nightstand, she smiled. But when she glimpsed her reflection in the cheval mirror, a wan face looked back at her with haunted eyes.

You have every right to be hurt and angry, an inner voice taunted. *Every right to be jealous of your brother's happiness. Every right to blame God for what happened to you.*

"No. I will never blame God for the wickedness of sinful human beings." She wanted to sink to her knees and beg God's forgiveness for even acknowledging such cold, ugly thoughts.

❧

Healy felt like he'd died and gone to heaven. Heaven couldn't be any sweeter than this, could it? Blueberry waffles dripping with melted butter, hot maple syrup sliding across a shiny china plate. Fresh-brewed coffee with a hint of cinnamon, and was that real cream in the little blue cow-shaped pitcher?

"Sorry the waffles are the frozen kind." Pastor Henke removed two more from the toaster oven and plopped them on Healy's plate. "Being a widower, I've chosen convenience over haute cuisine. More coffee? Orange juice?"

"Pastor, you've done too much already." Healy wasn't real sure what *haute cuisine* was, but these toaster waffles tasted mighty fine. He shoveled in another mouthful and groaned in delicious agony.

The white-haired gentleman filled a mug of coffee for himself and settled his bulk into a chair. "So, my dear boy, are you awake enough to finish that extraordinary tale you began in my office yesterday before the budget committee arrived?"

"Where'd I leave off?" Yesterday already seemed like a blur. Healy spread a pale yellow chunk of butter across the steamy waffles, then added more syrup.

"I believe you'd come to the part about seeing Zion's ad in the newspaper." Pastor Henke stirred cream into his coffee. "I'm still amazed you'd trek all the way to Aileen. Whatever possessed you, especially in this merciless heat?"

Fork poised above his plate, Healy stared thoughtfully. "Couldn't shake the feeling this is where God was sending me."

"You mentioned something about an old friend you were

hoping to find?"

"I'm afraid that's a lost cause." Healy exhaled long and loud. "Thought maybe that's why Aileen sounded familiar to me—maybe from a letter or something. Prison sorta messed with my memory. Some stuff I remember real well. Other stuff. . .it's just gone."

The phone jangled, and Pastor Henke jumped up to answer it. He stood with his back to Healy and spoke in muted tones. The best Healy could make out was the occasional "I see" and "Well, well, well."

Finally Pastor Henke said good-bye and turned to face Healy. His mouth formed a thin line. "That was the warden."

The waffles turned to cement at the bottom of Healy's stomach. He knew Pastor Henke had placed some calls to verify his story. Couldn't blame the man, considering the way Healy had walked in off the street, looking awful and smelling worse. Now the big question was, what exactly would the warden have said about him?

"Oh, my boy, my boy." Pastor Henke clucked his tongue and returned to his chair.

Healy pressed back from the table. "It's okay, Pastor. I'll be out of here in—"

"Young man." Pastor Henke seized Healy by the wrist. "You are not going anywhere. At least not until we find you suitable employment and a place to live."

"But—"

"No buts about it. Warden Smithers confirmed everything you've told me. He's faxing detailed reports and letters of recommendation—his own, plus several from the prison chaplain, psychiatrist, job counselor, your parole officer, and others." The pastor released Healy's wrist, then sat back and smiled. "Seems you made quite an impression during your stay as a guest of the Michigan correctional system, and they are more than delighted to help facilitate your new start in life."

All the air rushed out of Healy's lungs. He lifted his gaze to the ceiling. "Thank You, Jesus!"

"Now, where were we?" Pastor Henke folded his hands around his coffee mug. "Ah yes, you were about to tell me about this friend you're looking for."

"Best friend a guy could ever have. We went to high school together, played on the football team. He's the one who led me to Christ."

"And there's a chance he might live in Aileen?"

Healy chewed another mouthful of waffle. "Could be, or maybe he has family here. All I remember for sure is that I used to write to Tom at a St. Louis address, and he owned an Italian restaurant."

"Your friend's name is Tom? He owned an Italian restaurant?"

Healy looked up at the sudden quaver in the pastor's voice. "Tom Bishop, yes, sir."

"Oh dear." Pastor Henke slowly shook his head. "Oh, my dear, dear boy, it's possible I may have some terribly sad news for you."

four

As Valerie poured grape juice into a plastic Little Mermaid cup for Annie's afternoon snack, the warble of the kitchen phone startled her. Annoyed with herself, she took a couple of steadying breaths before answering.

"It's me again," came Pastor Henke's cheery voice. "I'm calling with the answer to your prayers."

Valerie laughed as she helped Annie scoot up to the table. "Which prayer would that be? The one for rain, or the one for naturally curly hair, or the one for—"

Pastor Henke guffawed. "I didn't know you had such a long list. No, the one I had in mind is locating another handyman to finish the painting job. . .along with anything else Connor may have in mind."

A relieved sigh burst from Valerie's lungs. "Pastor, that's wonderful!"

"May I bring him right over?"

"Now?" Anxiety tightened her stomach.

"If this isn't a good time. . ."

"It's not that." She pressed a hand to her temple. She knew Phil Garcia from church, and the various other workmen had been referred by trusted family friends. It hadn't occurred to her until this moment that finding a new painter on such short notice might also mean bringing a complete stranger into the house. "Pastor, is. . .is this person someone you know?"

"Actually, he's just arrived in town," the pastor said slowly. "I assure you, he has solid references. However, I'm afraid his pecuniary situation is a bit fragile—"

"His *what*?" Valerie couldn't help but laugh. Pastor Henke

had an amusing if sometimes annoying habit of tossing around his extensive vocabulary.

"Sorry, my dear." He gave an embarrassed laugh. "He's in a financial bind, and I know Connor has the apartment above the garage. I thought perhaps your brother might consider making living arrangements a part of the man's compensation."

She hesitated. "Pastor, it's not that I don't trust your judgment, but—"

"I assure you, this young man is a fine Christian with experience in carpentry and painting, not to mention all kinds of other skills." Pastor Henke sighed. "Valerie, my dear, this man's arrival in Aileen seems ordained by God to meet both your needs and his. Have no fears about him. I have thoroughly investigated his background and I trust him completely."

With great effort, Valerie pushed her concerns aside. She'd learned long ago that Pastor Henke's instincts about people were usually right on target. "All right," she said, expelling a sharp breath. "Bring him over and we'll see what we can work out."

Ending the call, she gazed out the window toward the garage, a carriage house in the old days. The long, narrow rooms above had been converted into a modern apartment by the previous owner and now held most of Valerie's belongings from the Ashton Brook Lane house, items she'd never found the strength to sort through, let alone part with. If someone were to move into the apartment, she'd have no choice but to face the daunting task.

Maybe the time had come. *Lord, give me the strength and courage I lack.*

Annie's tap on her wrist brought her back to the present. "Can we play a game now?"

"Sure, sweetie." By the time Valerie caught up with her niece in the den, Annie had all the parts to her Cooties game spread across the coffee table. Valerie eased down to sit cross-legged on the soft, shaggy carpet. "Oh boy, my favorite."

They were halfway through the game, with Annie's Cootie several body parts ahead of Valerie's, when she heard the distinctive rumble of Pastor Henke's red Mustang convertible. Moments afterward, the doorbell rang.

"Who's here?" Annie asked.

"Pastor Henke's bringing over a new painter." Valerie rose stiffly and aimed her index finger at Annie with mock severity. "Don't mess with my Cootie."

A quick peek through the curtains raised second thoughts about Pastor Henke's judgment. Damp, dishwater-blond hair curled over the collar of the stranger's ill-fitting plaid shirt. A razor nick showed dark red on his sunburned face. An ugly scar blazed up his left arm.

A memory clamped down on her heart, sending it racing. She tore herself away from the window.

The bell rang again. "Valerie dear, it's Pastor Henke."

This is ridiculous. She forced her breathing to slow, yet her hands still shook as she deactivated the alarm system. She flung open the door and marshaled all the cheerfulness she could manage. "Hello, Pastor. Please come in."

❧

Healy's first glimpse of the slender woman took his breath away. Her gray eyes sparkled with a brightness to rival the summer sunshine. She wore her pale blond hair pulled back from her face in a fancy clip. Long strands shimmered across the shoulders of her blue-flowered dress.

"Valerie dear, thank you for seeing us on such short notice." Pastor Henke and his companion stepped into the foyer. "This is Healy, the young man I told you about." He paused, cleared his throat. "Healy. . .Ferguson."

Healy held his breath, awaiting Valerie Bishop's reaction. If the pastor's story was true, Healy now stood before Tom's wife.

Correction, Tom's widow.

"Hello." Her tone held the merest suggestion of hesitation, but she gave no sign she'd recognized his name. According to Pastor Henke, Valerie had a few gaps in her memory as well.

When the pastor first came up with the idea of recommending Healy for the handyman's job, Healy wasn't so sure. Pastor Henke had glossed over the details of Tom's death, but he gave the impression Valerie still struggled with the aftermath. What if the sudden appearance of Tom's old buddy the ex-con were too much for her?

But Pastor Henke had already put in a call to Valerie's brother, and both had come to the conclusion that Healy's arrival was God's doing, that somehow, some way, Healy might turn out to be the catalyst for healing that Valerie's family and friends had been praying for.

She slowly extended her hand to Healy. "Pastor Henke tells me you're a jack-of-all-trades, which is what we desperately need around here." She nodded through open French doors toward a room with paint-spattered tarps covering the floor and furniture.

Healy glanced into the living room. "Yes, ma'am, I know a good bit about painting and carpentry. Problem is, I'm in sort of a transition period and don't have my own tools or supplies." He ran a finger around the collar of his shirt. At least two sizes too small, it was the best the elderly preacher could come up with. Pastor Henke had found the shirt, a pair of khakis, and clean socks in a barrel of clothing the church had collected for a homeless ministry.

"We'll arrange for whatever supplies you need," Valerie said. "I understand you also need a place to stay. We have an apartment over the garage, and I'm sure my brother would be willing to negotiate living arrangements as part of your compensation."

She folded her arms and looked away for a brief second. Her voice faded as she added, "I'm afraid it'll take some doing to make the apartment livable, though."

Her kind, honey-soft voice belied the uncertainty Healy read in her posture and expression. Even with a fresh change of clothes, Healy knew he still must look like a down-and-out drifter. He swallowed and met her gaze. "I don't need much, ma'am, and I know how to work hard. If you give me a chance, I promise I won't let you down."

She swept him with an appraising glance, and her gray eyes softened. "Pastor Henke seems to think you're just the man for the job, Mr. Ferguson, and he's never given me reason to question his judgment."

"I really appreciate this, Mrs. . . ."

"Bishop. But Valerie is just fine. I'm sure you'd like to see the apartment." She started down the hall.

Healy's heart flip-flopped. It was all coming back to him now. Tom had written about marrying a beautiful blond wisp of a girl named Valerie. Only with Tom's penchant for bestowing nicknames, he usually referred to her as "Lady V." And they'd chosen to live in St. Louis because his wife had family nearby. . .family in a little town called Aileen.

A tremor of grief rolled through him. He thrust out a hand and reached for the nearest wall.

Pastor Henke grabbed Healy's elbow. "Easy there, my boy."

Valerie turned and came toward him. "Are you all right? Can I get you some water?"

A tow-headed child appeared at the other end of the hallway. "I'm coloring now, Aunt Val. I already put my Cootie together without you." She started toward Healy and pointed at him with a fist full of crayons. "Are you gonna paint Daddy's wall?"

The little girl's questions helped Healy corral his thoughts. He knelt and smiled at her, offering his hand to shake. "Hi, there. My name's Healy. What's yours?"

Her smooth, tiny hand slipped into his calloused one. "My name is Annie Maureen Paige. I'm four and I live here. Where do you live?"

"Uh, well, I'm between addresses right now." He rose awkwardly, glancing at Valerie.

The little girl tugged at his pants leg. "Wanna help me color my picture?"

"Not now, Annie," Valerie said with a quiet laugh. "We're on our way to show Mr. Ferguson the garage apartment. I'll color with you when we finish."

"Don't forget!" Annie skipped through a doorway near the back of the house.

With a tentative smile, Valerie continued down the hall, stopping in the kitchen to select a set of keys from a drawer. Healy and the pastor followed her outside onto a shaded porch, where she halted suddenly, and Healy had to catch himself before he stumbled into her. His face hovered inches from the back of her beautiful blond head. The scent of honeysuckle, intensified by the heat, filled his nostrils.

"The apartment's up there." Her voice had risen a couple of notches, growing stretched and thin. "If you don't mind, Pastor, I'll let you show Mr. Ferguson around."

"I understand," the pastor said softly, taking the keys she offered. "This way, my boy."

Healy tried to keep pace as the older man marched across the lawn and up a flight of weathered stairs. He shuffled his feet while Pastor Henke unlocked the apartment. "Pastor, I'm still not sure this is a good idea. Working here, keeping quiet about my prison record, and knowing Tom—any of it."

The door creaked open, and Pastor Henke pocketed the keys. "In this particular instance, I am relying on the wisdom of Ecclesiastes—'a time to be silent and a time to speak.' And for now, dear boy, this is the time to be silent. When the time is right to tell Valerie who you really are and where you came from, you'll know it."

Pastor Henke flipped a light switch and illuminated the narrow kitchenette to the right of the door. Dust-covered boxes lined the floor and countertops. Healy moistened his lips. "You never finished telling me. What. . .happened to Tom? How exactly did he die?"

"Ah, Healy, it's a heartbreaking story, so hard to talk about." The pastor strode to a streaked window overlooking the driveway and forced it open. "There, perhaps we can air this place out a bit."

Sweat trickled down Healy's ribcage. He could feel wetness spreading under his armpits. "I need to know, Pastor. He was my best friend."

"I know, dear boy, I know. As I said, it was not quite five years ago—October, as I recall. Tom and Valerie had just closed their restaurant for the evening." Pastor Henke shoved a crate out of the way and opened a door at the far end of the living room. "Here's the bedroom. Not large, but a nice view, don't you think? And it has a good-sized closet."

"More than enough room for my stuff. . .if it ever shows up again. Go on, Pastor."

Pastor Henke opened another window, then dabbed his reddened face with a folded handkerchief. "It was a vicious, senseless, tragic accident. Tom was. . .he was killed by a speeding car."

Stricken, Healy pretended to examine the tiny bathroom. He turned on the sink faucet, and brown water gushed out.

"Oh dear, rusty pipes," Pastor Henke said, peering over Healy's shoulder. "Valerie was also injured in the accident, and after she left the hospital, her brother and his wife brought her to live with them."

Healy met the pastor's gaze in the bathroom mirror. "She was there when it happened?"

"Sad indeed. But Valerie has truly been a blessing to the Paige family, and to everyone at Zion Community Church who has gotten to know her. She still has much to overcome, but I've never met a more generous, more loving, more forgiving person."

Staring at his own reflection, Healy glimpsed the deep

lines etched around his eyes. So much sorrow, so much pain to absorb in one short day.

※

Valerie pressed a glass to the refrigerator spigot and watched clear, cold water pour out. Would this heat never break? Connor would have to hold his Fourth of July barbecue indoors, or his guests would collapse from heatstroke.

She curled her fingers around the frosty water glass and glanced out the window. Pastor Henke and the handyman must be sweltering in the airless apartment. Even if they thought to turn on the air conditioners, it would take hours to cool the place down. And if the new handyman planned to move in anytime soon, she—or someone—faced a huge, hot cleanup job. At least he could use Valerie's furniture and dishes and such. Someone might as well, since she began to doubt she'd ever be the one residing in the apartment. She suspected the man owned little more than the clothes on his back and could only wonder about the circumstances that had brought him to Pastor Henke. When the time was right, maybe he'd tell her more about himself. In the meantime, she'd try to be as kind and compassionate as she knew how.

Sympathy welled for Healy Ferguson—and yet it was more than mere pity she felt for him. A kindred spirit, perhaps? Someone as bound by a difficult past as she?

True, when she first saw him, icy fingers of panic had tightened around her throat. Not that he reminded her so much of *him*, the face that still haunted her nights more frequently than she wanted to admit. But *he* had a scar, too.

"Of course, the scar." She mentally chided herself. "Lord, forgive me for judging a man because he has a scar."

He could have gotten it anywhere. Probably in his carpentry work, with a sharp tool of some kind. A scar didn't make a man a criminal.

Annie danced into the kitchen. "I finished coloring. I made the tree blue and the apples purple. Isn't that silly?" She cocked her head and laughed. "Where's Pastor and that man?"

"Still looking at the apartment." Valerie knelt to give Annie a hug. The gesture reminded her that Healy had also knelt when introducing himself to Annie. She pictured the gentleness—the *guilelessness*—in his eyes, and the trusting way Annie had taken to him immediately.

How could Valerie not like a man who understood so instinctively how to relate to a child?

five

"Well?" Valerie poured glasses of iced tea and placed them before Pastor Henke and Healy Ferguson. "Is it utterly hopeless up there, or can we make the apartment livable?"

"It's a fine place." Healy stared at his hands, wrapped around the glass. "A lot more space than what I'm used to."

"I'm sure it will clean up nicely," Pastor Henke said.

"That'll be the fun part." Valerie's teasing tone masked the choking dread that threatened to close her throat. She turned to the refrigerator and exhaled slowly. "How about some milk for you, Annie?"

"Yes, please." Annie scooted her chair closer to Healy's. "Are you gonna live in our 'partment?"

He took a long drink of tea. "I sure would like to, but the decision's up to your aunt and your parents."

Valerie set a plate of oatmeal raisin cookies on the table and settled into a chair. "Sorry, these aren't homemade. I was a business major, never much good in the kitchen." She twisted her wedding band and smiled over the bittersweet memories.

"Valerie my dear," Pastor Henke began, "I did a bit of snooping upstairs. I came across some boxes of men's clothing that might fit Healy. I wondered—"

Healy looked suddenly flustered. "No, Pastor, I couldn't. I can get by for now."

"It's. . .it's all right." Valerie had kept Tom's things boxed away long enough. Besides, if Tom were alive, he'd give the shirt off his back to help someone in need. To honor her husband's memory, she could do no less.

"Please," she said, squaring her shoulders, "it would make

me very happy to see my husband's things put to good use by someone who needs them. Take whatever you need."

Healy murmured a hoarse "Thank you."

Valerie nibbled on a cookie, feeling as if at least a tiny portion of her immense burden had lifted. It was a small step, finally letting go of some of the tangible reminders of the past, but an important one.

In the ensuing silence, she returned her attention to Healy. He reached for a cookie with a hesitant tremor, like a child who feared a slap on the hand for taking something he shouldn't. She had the feeling the tall, lean man had received few breaks in his life.

Lord, he looks as if he could use some friends. Let me be one.

She glanced at the clock. "It'll be at least another hour before Ellen and Connor get home. In the meantime, Mr. Ferguson—"

He held up a hand and gave an awkward laugh. " 'Mister' doesn't quite fit, if you know what I mean. Ferguson, or Healy, or just plain 'hey, you' is more what I'm used to."

Valerie looked at him appraisingly. What this man needed more than anything was a heaping dose of self-respect. "Then I'll use your first name, Healy, because that's what a friend would call you. And with that in mind, you can drop the 'ma'am' with me. It's Valerie, okay?"

His voice dropped to barely a whisper. "That'll be just fine, ma'am—I mean, Valerie."

"Good." She nodded firmly and rose to refill his iced tea glass. "What I started to say was, why don't you take another look around the apartment? Help yourself to whatever clothes you can wear. And if you end up staying, feel free to use the dishes, furniture, linens, whatever."

"Yes, go take another look around, Healy," Pastor Henke said. "I have some church business I need to talk with Valerie about."

"Um, okay, if you're sure."

"Here, take some tea and cookies with you." Valerie wrapped three cookies in a napkin. "And turn the air conditioner on, first thing."

When the back door clicked shut, Valerie turned to Pastor Henke. "He seems enormously shy, but. . .there's something special about him, something that makes me trust him." Taking her chair, she ran a fingernail along the edge of the table. "I hope Connor will feel the same way."

The pastor cast her a knowing smile. "I'm sure he will."

"I like him," Annie said. "He looks kinda like the prince in my storybook."

Valerie recalled her first glimpse of Healy Ferguson outside the front door. Although she might call him attractive in a rugged sort of way, *prince* would not have been her first choice of words. The man obviously carried deeper scars than the one visible across his arm.

"I can tell he's had a difficult life, Pastor," she said. "Do you know how he got that ugly scar?"

The white-haired man cleared his throat. "I believe he said it happened with a knife."

She couldn't suppress a sardonic laugh. "I hope it doesn't mean he's another accident-prone handyman."

"Oh no, it wasn't his fault," the pastor said quickly. He coughed again. "Er, do you mind if we change the subject briefly? I was hoping to convince you to take over as the congregation's prayer-chain coordinator."

Valerie touched a hand to her cheek in surprise. "Is Catherine Higgins resigning?"

"Not exactly. The church council is going to kindly suggest that she take a much deserved rest. The truth is, Catherine is getting a bit too hard of hearing for the job." He chuckled. "Never did get it straight that we needed to pray for healing for Howard Nelson's gout—not his *goat*."

Valerie burst out in giggles. "I could barely keep from laughing out loud when she called saying Howard's goat was ailing. I didn't even know the Nelsons had a goat."

"They don't." Pastor Henke's sides shook with laughter. He patted his folded handkerchief to his forehead and exhaled loudly. "So, are you up for the position?"

She thought a moment, remembering the many friends at Zion who had visited and prayed with her over the past few years. It would be a way to give back to them some of the love she had received. Even better, if not exactly the reason Pastor Henke and her family would like to hear, she could handle the responsibilities without ever leaving the house.

"Sounds like it's right up my alley," she said. "When do I start?"

ea

Healy stood amid the boxes of Tom's things and let grief wash over him. He lifted a maroon polo shirt and imagined how Tom's broad shoulders must have filled it out. His fists knotted around the coarse cotton fabric. *Lord, why? Why'd You bring me all this way, only to let me find out my best friend is dead?*

Pastor Henke appeared at the door, carrying a plastic tote containing cleaning supplies. "Valerie thought you might want to start getting the place habitable."

Healy shook off his grief. "Thanks. Good idea."

While they cleaned and sorted, the pastor told Healy a little more about the Paige family and their association with Zion. "Connor's an elder, and Ellen was leading a ladies' Bible study until she passed the baton to Bonnie Trapp last spring."

"And Valerie?" Healy's question was muffled by the stack of musty-smelling beige towels he carried to the bathroom.

"As a matter of fact, she just agreed to be our new prayer-chain coordinator." Pastor Henke clucked his tongue. "A worthy vocation, but such a waste when she could be doing so much more."

Healy's heart clenched with concern for his friend's widow. The moment he first laid eyes on her, he'd felt strong protective impulses rising from deep within his bones. He'd do anything, dare anything, if he could ease her sorrow and erase the fear that lurked behind those shimmering gray eyes.

Within the hour, a blue sedan drove up, and the floor beneath Healy's feet vibrated as the automatic garage door rumbled open.

"That's Ellen," Pastor Henke announced. "I'll just run down and say hello. Be back shortly."

A few minutes later, Healy saw a silver minivan park in the driveway. A tall man dressed in an expensive-looking gray suit got out, unlocked the side gate, and entered the backyard. The man took three steps toward the house only to snap his fingers, spin on one heel, and trot back to the gate to lock it securely.

Healy could only shake his head at such paranoia—bolted doors, locked gates, alarm systems. Poor Tom. Poor Valerie. He shunted his gnawing grief aside with more vigorous cleaning efforts. It seemed forever before the pastor returned.

"The Paiges are home," Pastor Henke called from the landing. "Time to meet your future employer."

The slender, sandy-haired man who'd arrived in the mini-van met them at the back door of the house.

"Hi. Connor Paige. Come on in." Though he'd removed his suit coat, his pastel blue dress shirt and loosened tie easily fit Healy's image of a successful surgeon—and made Healy feel more out of place than ever.

With a sweaty palm he shook the doctor's hand. "Healy Ferguson. How do you do, sir?"

"Mr. Ferguson. Nice to meet you." Connor introduced his wife, Ellen, an attractive woman with a cap of short brown curls. She towered over the petite Valerie Bishop, who waited nearby wearing an encouraging smile. The little girl, Annie, knelt on a kitchen chair, printing her name over and over on a sheet of lined paper.

"Have a seat." Connor motioned Healy toward the table,

and they sat down. "Pastor Henke explained about your need for work and a place to live. So you have a good bit of handyman experience?"

"Yes, sir." *In a manner of speaking.* Prison vocational training and work assignments, then a year on parole working for a building contractor, ought to count for something. Healy took the chair next to Annie. Though he knew Pastor Henke had already spoken at length with the doctor, the man still seemed uncomfortably formal and reserved. Healy mentally prepared himself in case Dr. Paige decided to send him on his way.

And then his nostrils picked up an enticing aroma coming from the stove. His stomach gave an ominous grumble, and he clamped an arm across his waist.

Ellen's chuckle eased his embarrassment. "Hmm, sounds like somebody's hungry. Don't worry, Mr. Ferguson, you're invited to supper. You, too, Pastor. We have plenty." She went to the stove to stir the contents of a large stockpot.

Pastor Henke released a disappointed moan. "How kind of you to ask, but I'm afraid I can't stay." He glanced at his watch. "In fact, I'm late already for another appointment. I'll leave Healy in your care."

"But, Pastor—" Healy started from his chair. Lowering his voice, he said, "What if this doesn't work out after all? What if—"

The pastor winked. "Where's your faith, my boy?" To the Paige family he said, "I'll see myself out. Have a good evening, all."

Healy could hardly swallow as he sank into his chair. "I, uh. . .I guess I'm stuck here for a while."

"I should certainly hope so," Ellen said, "since you're our replacement handyman." She measured out a fistful of dry spaghetti and dropped it into another stockpot. Steam swirled around her, mirroring the haze of disbelief filling Healy's mind.

Connor pushed his chair back. "Healy, would you join me in my study? It might be easier to discuss the details of this arrangement in private."

All right, Ferguson, get ready for the ax to fall.

He followed the doctor down the hallway into a paneled office lined with bookshelves. Through partially open wooden blinds, the evening sun sketched a ladder-like pattern across the massive desk. The men took seats across the desk from each other, and Healy caught the look of uncertainty in Connor Paige's eyes.

The doctor spoke slowly. "As I'm sure you know, when Pastor Henke phoned me earlier, he told me all about your time in prison."

"Yes, sir." Healy pressed his hands together. "I made a serious mistake, one I'll regret the rest of my life. But I'm not the same person I was sixteen years ago. I'm just praying now to put the past behind me and make a new start."

"I admire you for that." Connor rested his forearms on the desk. "But I'll admit, when Pastor Henke told me his idea, I had my doubts. The faxes from the prison officials, your parole officer, and former employer helped a lot, but what clinched it for me was learning you're Tom's friend Gus. He used to talk about you often, and I know he'd want me to help you any way I can."

"Thank you, sir. Tom was the only real friend I ever had. I can't believe he's dead."

"I'm sorry. We've had over four years to grieve. You've only just found out."

Healy nodded, unable to speak.

After a moment of silence, Connor went on. "I agree with Pastor Henke—your arrival in town may well be the answer to our prayers, in more ways than one. But since Valerie obviously doesn't remember you, I'd rather not tell her anything just yet about your connection to Tom, and especially not about your prison record. My goal is to get her back into therapy soon, and I don't want to do anything to rock the boat until I'm certain she's getting better." Connor rubbed his chin. "It goes against my nature to keep things from my wife, but at this point, I'm not planning to tell Ellen, either. She and Val talk about everything, and I'm afraid Ellen might unintentionally let something slip."

Healy nodded. "I understand. I'll abide by whatever you say."

Connor's eyes narrowed. "But let me make something perfectly clear. If you give me even the smallest reason to doubt your sincerity or your integrity, I'll personally buy your bus ticket back to where you came from." He reached for a yellow legal pad. "Now, let's discuss the working arrangements."

As Connor finished outlining the next few projects he had in mind, his little daughter came to summon them to dinner. Joining the family at the table, Healy smiled his thanks as Ellen Paige set a plate of spaghetti in front of him, next to a bowl of green salad. The marinara sauce and Italian spices smelled incredible.

Connor folded his hands. "Healy, it's our custom to offer thanks before each meal."

"If I may be so forward, sir, I've got a lot to be thankful for today and I wonder if you'd let me ask the blessing."

Connor looked at him with mild surprise. "By all means."

Stealing a glance at the slender, flaxen-haired woman across the table, Healy began, "Precious Lord, how do I thank You for such bounteous care? I came to this town on faith and a prayer, and look how You have rewarded me. What an awesome God You are. Bless this family, bless Pastor Henke, and bless this food to the nourishment of our bodies. In Jesus' name, amen."

A soft chorus of "amens" sounded around the table.

"How's the apartment coming?" Valerie twirled strands of spaghetti around her fork. "Did it ever cool off up there?"

"Took awhile, but it's comfortable now." He paused to

savor the rich flavors dancing across his tongue. "I cannot remember when I've tasted anything so good."

Ellen sprinkled freshly grated Parmesan over her spaghetti and passed the container to Healy. "The recipe came from Valerie's late husband's family."

Healy nodded. "From Italy, I—" *I remember,* he'd almost said. He sensed Connor's warning glance. "I mean, this is such great Italian food, his family had to have been Italian."

Valerie smiled, sadness crinkling the corners of her eyes. "Tom's maternal grandmother was Italian. Grandma Carmela taught him everything she knew about cooking, even helped get our restaurant started—while I stayed out of the way and kept the books. Thank goodness Ellen has the talent and patience to recreate the family recipes. My attempts always flop."

Healy poked at his salad, stabbing a mushroom and tomato onto the end of his fork. She seemed to talk easily enough about Tom. And yet he'd been warned she still couldn't venture past the backyard without the effort triggering an anxiety attack.

Father, help me not to do anything to upset Valerie. That's the last thing I'd ever want to do. And I know Tom must be there in heaven with You, so make sure he knows it, too.

Someday, when the time was right, Healy prayed God would allow him to tell her himself about his friendship with Tom, before a chance discovery or someone's slip of the tongue revealed the truth by accident.

Yet the thought of her knowing terrified him, because telling Valerie the truth would also mean revealing the fact that he'd spent fifteen years in prison for manslaughter.

six

Valerie watched from the living room doorway as Healy lined up the last strip of an elegant rose-print wallpaper border. The first time she'd seen him wearing one of Tom's old T-shirts, her heart had twisted, but day by day it had grown easier, especially knowing Tom's things were being put to good use.

She stepped into the room. "A little higher on that end— perfect."

With expert strokes Healy smoothed the border above the fruitwood-stained chair rail, trimmed the edge, and rolled the seams. He stepped back to appraise his work and expelled a long breath. "That should do it. The living room's done."

Valerie clapped her hands in delight. "This calls for a celebration. How about an ice-cold lemonade?"

"Let me clean up in here first. Join you in the kitchen in a few minutes?"

"I'll have it ready and waiting." She cast a smile over her shoulder and sauntered down the hall.

Pastor Henke had not overstated Healy's abilities in the handyman department. He'd already finished painting and papering the living room, fixed a leaky faucet in the powder room, stopped an annoying stair step from creaking, and replaced a cracked tile on the kitchen counter.

And all this on top of cleaning and organizing the garage apartment. She regretted being unable to help him sort through all the crates and extra furniture stored up there— most of it was hers, after all—but no amount of good intentions or willpower had been able to propel her across the backyard and up those stairs.

She recalled the verse from 1 John she had clung to so often: "Perfect love drives out fear." Yet despite daily prayer and several failed attempts at therapy, she couldn't seem to make it true for herself.

How much longer, Father? Why is my faith so weak that I can't overcome this?

She had just filled two glasses with lemonade when Healy came through the kitchen, carrying his wallpapering supplies. Tucking a leftover roll of paper under his chin, he reached for the knob to let himself out the back door. As he pulled it open, the warning beep of the security system caught Valerie's attention.

"Oh no, hold on." She rushed over to enter the code before the alarm sounded.

Healy let out a frustrated groan. "Sorry, I keep forgetting."

"It's my fault." Her face warmed. "I just feel safer when the alarm is set."

She locked the door behind him but resisted her compulsion to reset the alarm. "He's coming right back, silly," she told herself, but it didn't keep the apprehension from rising in her throat. She watched for Healy to return from the garage. When she saw him climb the porch steps, she silently unlocked the door and strode back to the table.

"Cold lemonade, as promised." She closed her eyes in gratitude when he remembered to lock the door and set the alarm. "You must think I'm so paranoid." Her forced laugh sounded hollow. "It's a long story."

Healy took the chair across from her and downed a long gulp of lemonade. The awkward silence between them grew.

"The munchkin still napping?" Healy finally asked.

"Mm-hmm." Valerie sipped her drink.

He chuckled. "Figured. Otherwise she'd be in here asking for cookies."

"You've got that right." She felt herself relaxing. "You're so good with Annie. You must really like kids."

"My, uh, buddies where I came from—some of them had kids. I was always a bit envious."

Did his hand shake just now as he lifted his glass?

"You don't talk much about where you came from."

"Not much to tell."

She noticed his sunburned cheeks and nose had started to peel. "I don't mean to pry. I just wondered. . ."

"I'm from up north." His gaze met hers, and he exhaled slowly. "How about you?"

"I grew up in Boston." She swirled the ice in her glass. "My mother still lives there. I'll bet she's having a much cooler summer than we are."

"This heat's the worst I've ever known. What's the deal, anyway?"

Valerie gave him a conspiratorial wink. "I think the weather forecasters made some kind of deal with the air conditioner manufacturers."

"Ah, I see." Healy laughed, and she joined him, relieved to see the troubled look leave his eyes.

She liked this man more every day, shyness and all. Healy was clearly a man of integrity and great patience, someone whose character had been carved out of trials and pain, not unlike her own. She wasn't entirely sure when the pity she had first felt for him had shifted to friendly concern, and then from concern to genuine interest.

Truth be told, she wasn't exactly sure how to interpret her feelings for the Paiges' inscrutable new handyman. She only knew she wanted to get to know him better. . .much, much better.

❧

The rumble of a car caused Healy to look up from his supper of macaroni and cheese. From the apartment window he saw the elderly Pastor Henke emerge from his flashy red Mustang. He couldn't help but chuckle at the incongruity.

Moments later, heavy footsteps shook the outside stairs,

and Pastor Henke's round face appeared through the glass in the door.

"Hey, Pastor, come on in."

"Oh dear, I'm interrupting your dinner. I just came by with this." Pastor Henke held out Healy's scruffy, stained duffel bag.

"My stuff." Healy grinned in surprise. He'd braved a call to the police department a few days ago and learned the thief was caught when he tried to rob another traveler. A search of his apartment turned up a whole stash of luggage, including Healy's duffel bag and all its contents—short the twenty-dollar bill, unfortunately. Pastor Henke had a friend in the department who kindly intervened to speed up the release of Healy's property from the evidence room.

"Sorry I couldn't fetch this for you sooner, but things at church became rather hectic this week." A distracted look crossed the pastor's face.

"Thanks, I really appreciate it." Healy set the bag on a cushioned armchair in the sitting area. Returning to the table, he cast an awkward glance at his meager meal. "I don't have much to offer, but you're welcome to join me."

"A glass of ice water would be most welcome." Pastor Henke took a chair at the end of the small gray Formica table. "Please, go ahead and eat before it gets cold."

Healy placed a frosty tumbler before the pastor and self-consciously resumed eating. "Valerie and the Paiges have been real nice about inviting me to take meals with them, but I feel like I'm imposing."

"I'm sure they don't think so. Tell me, how is everything going?"

"Real well." Healy swallowed his last bite and pushed the plate away. "It's good work for good people. I can't thank you enough for making this possible."

"Connor told me at church Sunday that you're doing an excellent job." The pastor gave a half smile and leaned forward. "Of course, Phil Garcia fears you'll steal away all his clients while he's incapacitated with his broken leg."

Healy shot the pastor a worried glance. "Please, I wouldn't—"

"My boy, I'm only teasing. No, no, there's plenty of work in the area to keep Phil and you and any number of handymen amply employed for years to come."

Feeling stupid, Healy sat back and shook his head. "Whoa, I'm almost as paranoid as Valerie."

Pastor Henke grew quiet. "Yes, it's a shame, isn't it?"

Healy gave a huff. "I don't know how many times I've accidentally set off the burglar alarm. Once the cops even came out. I thought I'd have a heart attack right then and there."

Pastor Henke tapped his index finger lightly on the tabletop. "Valerie is still unaware of your past?"

"Connor warned me not to tell her yet. She seems frightened of enough stuff as it is." He pushed back from the table and braced his forearms on his thighs. "Pastor, seeing her so scared all the time. . .it grates on my soul."

The pastor stared at his brown wingtips. "As it does with all of us."

Healy tried to reconcile his impression of Valerie as usually competent and self-controlled with the image the pastor and Connor had painted of a woman reduced to a mass of raw nerves after the death of her husband. "If she's that bad off, how does she manage so well taking care of the house and watching over Annie? I mean. . ."

Pastor Henke narrowed his eyes. "You mean, how can Connor and Ellen entrust their child to someone so unstable?"

Healy's throat closed. He nodded without meeting the pastor's gaze.

"They didn't right away, of course." The pastor sipped his iced tea. "Annie was born a few months after Tom died. Ellen had already planned to take a couple of years off from teaching, so she also used the time to assist in Valerie's recovery.

We all soon realized that Valerie needed to feel *needed*. She has a great fondness for children, and Annie became the center of her world. More and more frequently, Ellen left the child in Valerie's care for short trips to run errands and such, and Valerie's confidence blossomed."

"But suppose something happened. I mean, if she can't even leave the house. . ."

"Connor and Ellen introduced Valerie to several trusted neighbors who are usually home during the day. In addition, she's always had a list of friends from church she can call." Pastor Henke folded his hands on the table. "And she is not incompetent, my boy, simply haunted by a terrible trauma."

Healy still fought to grasp the reality of Tom's death. No one seemed willing to talk about the details, but he had to know. "Please, Pastor, tell me more about the accident."

"If you insist." The pastor sadly shook his head. "That night three men had just robbed a convenience store, and the police were chasing them. For some reason Valerie has never remembered, instead of Tom's going straight to their car in the lot next to the restaurant, he was crossing the street."

Cold dread snaked through Healy's gut. He bowed his head. "Oh, blessed Jesus."

The pastor raked a hand through his thinning hair. His gaze held a faraway look. "Tom was hit by the robbers' getaway car. It spun out of control and smashed into a light pole, and the three men tried to escape on foot. Valerie was grabbed and shoved by one of them and had to be hospitalized with severe injuries. As for the rest of the details, her mind is a blank. Police arrived within moments and captured the men."

"Where are they now?" Healy asked through tight lips.

"In prison, for a long, long time."

"Good."

❧

Valerie massaged her back as she settled into her desk chair.

She hadn't written in her journal for almost a week now, and her conscience stung. How could she be so neglectful?

Turning to a fresh page, she uncapped her fountain pen and stared into the darkness outside her window. A smile curled her lips as an image of Tom's face formed in her mind's eye.

Then the clean-cut dark hair of her memories paled to a shaggy dishwater blond, the blue eyes turned hazel, and it became Healy's face she pictured, not Tom's. A stab of shame shot through her, but in that moment she could almost hear Tom's voice: *"It's okay, Lady V, I don't blame you. It's all right to move on."*

If only she could. The events of one dreadful night had altered her life forever. With each passing year her hopes of feeling safe and whole again slid further and further away.

She turned to the open journal and lifted her pen.

My dearest,

I still miss you so much—all the joy we might have had—and this is the only place I can come to when I want to be with you. When I see Connor and Ellen's happiness, I only miss you more. I wish I could hold you in my arms just once and tell you how much I love you.

You would like Healy. Annie adores him, and early in the mornings, before it gets too terribly hot, he pushes her in the swing or plays hide-and-seek with her in the backyard. They have such wonderful fun together.

Oh, my love, I wish you could have stayed. I cling to God's promise that someday we will be together in heaven.

She heard a light tapping on the door and quietly closed the journal. "Come in."

"Hi, Val." Ellen stepped into the room. "Am I interrupting?"

"Not at all." She rose to greet her sister-in-law with a hug. "How have you been feeling?"

Ellen sank onto an ice-blue velveteen loveseat. "Tired, mostly. And the morning sickness is kicking in."

"I heard you in the bathroom this morning. Is it really bad?"

"When is throwing up ever fun?" Ellen looked toward the ceiling. "Connor's such an angel, wanting to hover and mop my brow, but when I'm hanging over the commode, in the words of Greta Garbo, 'I vant to be alone.'" She picked up a throw pillow and pressed it to her stomach. "Ugh! It's so. . .humiliating. Mind if we change the subject?"

Valerie chuckled and sat down beside her. "Be my guest."

"Healy's amazing, isn't he? I can't believe all he's done already."

"I know. All I have to do is mention something needs doing, and before I know it, he's finished."

"So, now that the downstairs is in good shape, what should we have Healy work on next?" Ellen's appraising gaze swept from floor to ceiling. "We've done hardly anything in here since you moved in, except slap on a coat of paint and hang curtains."

Valerie shifted sideways and faced Ellen. "Wouldn't you rather fix up the extra bedroom for the new baby's nursery?"

"We have time." She chewed her lip. "You really need some bookshelves. There's room for built-ins between those two windows."

Valerie traced a leaf in the pattern of her capris. "Ellen, what do you think of Healy—I mean, other than as an excellent handyman?"

"He's hard to get to know, but I've liked him from the start. I'm still vague about how Pastor Henke found him."

A twinge of longing gripped Valerie's heart. "Healy sure doesn't talk much, does he?"

Ellen leaned toward her with a probing stare. "What is that look I see in your eyes, Valerie Bishop? Are you getting interested in our tall, handsome stranger?"

"Whatever gave you such an idea?" Rising abruptly, Valerie

strode across the room. Why did she feel so jumpy all of a sudden?

"Well, you two do spend a lot of time together."

"He's working, and I'm supervising. I think you could say we're becoming friends, but I don't know him nearly well enough to even consider being *interested* in him."

Ellen rose and paced the room, nodding and casting sidelong glances at Valerie. "Yes, I think we need to have Healy start on this room next. Bookshelves for sure—or if he can do it, maybe some glass-front curio cabinets. And I'll pick up some wallpaper books and paint swatches after classes tomorrow." She winked. "That should keep both of you busy for the next few weeks."

Valerie looked heavenward and laughed. "Ellen, you are impossible."

When her sister-in-law excused herself for bed, Valerie collapsed onto the loveseat. She sighed as Healy's face filled her mind once more. "Lord, I have to admit, there is something about the man."

Fair-skinned and lean, he certainly had little in common with Tom, the muscular, raven-haired ex-football jock she'd fallen in love with in college. Tom had been loud, vivacious, even a prankster at times.

Healy, on the other hand, seemed unusually quiet and reserved. She'd caught only glimpses of his playful side when he spent time with Annie, but even those rare moments warmed something inside her.

"Who am I kidding?" Such thoughts could lead nowhere, not as long as she remained trapped inside a house with an activated security system, hidden behind a high privacy fence with a padlocked gate. Not as long as she feared her own shadow.

She pressed her fingertips to her brimming eyes. "Please, Father, let me live like a normal person. Take away the pain of *that night* and let me heal."

seven

Valerie closed the oven door on a tray of brown-and-serve wheat rolls—the only cooking task her brother and sister-in-law would entrust to her—and hurried to make a space on the kitchen table for the steaming meat platter Connor had just brought in from the grill. The pungent aroma of mesquite-smoked beef brisket, chicken, and sausage set her taste buds aquiver. She pinched off a bite of brisket and popped it into her mouth.

"Hey, no nibbling." Conner slapped her hand.

"But the temptation is simply irresistible." She snuck another bite and danced away. Savoring the morsel, she narrowed her eyes. "Why, brother dear, is that a trace of barbecue sauce on *your* upper lip?"

Ellen entered from the hall, followed by sounds of laughter and conversation. "Everyone loves what we've done with the house. Mmm, yummy." She snagged a chicken wing.

"Enough, you two." Connor dragged a napkin across his mouth. "Save some for our guests."

Ellen cast him an innocent smile. "But, honey, I'm eating for two."

The oven timer beeped. Donning quilted mitts, Valerie brought out the rolls and slid them into the cloth-lined basket Ellen offered. "Looks like everything's ready."

"Great. I'll announce dinner." Ellen headed toward the dining room with the basket of rolls.

Connor lifted the meat platter. "Isn't Healy coming? I haven't seen him all evening."

"I told him several times he was invited." Valerie parted the window curtains. Behind the garage apartment, the evening

58

sky blazed purple and orange—probably the only fireworks she'd see tonight. She turned away abruptly. "Maybe Healy's uncomfortable about being with so many people he doesn't know."

"Wouldn't surprise me. Well, I'm starved. We're eating now, with or without Healy." He marched out of the kitchen.

Biting her lip, Valerie pulled open the back door and stepped onto the porch. She'd managed four quick steps across the lawn when the inevitable rush of panic swept through her. What if the gates were unlocked? What if someone had crept into the backyard and lay in wait behind a bush or tree?

Her heart raced. She couldn't breathe. Every sound seemed amplified a hundred times. She dare not turn around and run back inside—someone might grab her from behind. Yet she couldn't move forward, couldn't seem to move at all.

God, help me.

"There you are," came Connor's voice from the porch. Instantly he appeared beside her, his protective arms encircling her. "You okay, sis?"

She relaxed against him. "I wanted to try again to convince Healy to come to dinner. But I couldn't get there."

Connor gently turned her toward the house. "You tried, that's what counts."

Her jaw clenched. "It's not enough."

"I know I promised not to push, but I wish you'd try counseling again."

"If it didn't work before, what makes you think things would be different now?"

"We could try other doctors, a different approach. I've read about some new medications—"

Reaching the porch, Valerie stopped and faced her brother with pleading eyes. "Listen to me, Con, I simply can't bear the idea of reliving everything, being prodded to fill in the missing pieces. And I don't want to go through life depending on drugs. I did that for too long after I got out of the hospital, and it almost turned my brain to mush. Please, let me handle this my own way." She reached for the doorknob. "And pray for me."

ᵃ₈

All afternoon Healy had been inhaling the mouth-watering aromas drifting upward from the Paiges' backyard. He'd never smelled anything as tantalizing as beef sizzling over glowing mesquite embers. From his kitchen window he'd watched a sweat-soaked Connor brave the midsummer heat and the even higher temperatures of the smoky grill.

But he'd seen little of Valerie today and assumed she must be busy in the house, helping Ellen prepare for the party.

And he missed her. More than he dared acknowledge.

Hardly a day had passed in the last two weeks when he hadn't spent at least several hours in her presence. Their conversations were pretty much limited to painting and wall-papering and carpentry, but just being in the same room with her made him feel. . .

Admit it. She makes you feel like a man.

For sixteen years he'd felt lower than the lowest animal. In prison he'd run the gamut of emotions, starting with intense remorse over the incident that had put him there. Self-loathing finally gave way to fleeting glimmers of hope that, with God's help, he just might survive the prison experience, maybe even come through it a better, stronger person.

Best of all, he eventually found himself able to accept the forgiveness in Christ that for so long Tom had tried to convince him could be his for the asking. And in that moment everything changed forever.

But he also had to accept that sin has its consequences. Prison did something to a man. The daily indignities—lack of privacy, the guards' insults, the brutal cruelty of fellow inmates—no matter how secure he felt in God's love, a part of him still hearkened to the murmurs of inferiority and unworthiness.

He settled into the armchair and reached for his Bible. The aging leather felt rough and dry, even in his calloused hands. Smudged fingerprints marred the once white pages, and penciled notes filled the margins. He'd written to Tom awhile ago, telling him how glad he was that his friend couldn't see how dirty and worn the Bible had grown.

"Just means you're using it," Tom had written back, *"and that's a good thing, Gus. Keep it up. I'm praying for you."*

"Aw, Tom." Healy's throat closed with grief as the Bible fell open to the flyleaf. "I can't believe you're dead. Going on five years, and I never knew."

For the millionth time his gaze fell upon Tom's inscription:

To Gus, my best friend and the best placekicker I ever blocked for. When things get tough and you can't see the end, read Joel 2:23–26. God is the great Restorer. No matter what happens, trust in Him.

Tom

The passage from the book of Joel had come to hold great meaning for Healy as the years of his sentence dragged by. He loved the images of God sending the autumn rains, the threshing floors filled with grain, the vats overflowing with new wine and oil.

Most of all, he clung to God's promise: "I will repay you for the years the locusts have eaten. . . . You will have plenty to eat, until you are full, and you will praise the name of the Lord your God, who has worked wonders for you; never again will my people be shamed."

Above the drone of the air conditioner he heard the *pop-pop-pop* of firecrackers. He went to the front window and looked out. Beyond the treetops, the darkened horizon lit up momentarily with a dazzle of green and gold.

Fireworks. He hadn't seen a real Fourth of July fireworks display since he was a teenager. He grinned like a kid as another sparkling spectacle of light mushroomed above the tree line.

Voices from below caught his attention. Down by the street he saw Connor, Ellen, and Annie along with several party guests setting up lawn chairs. His heart quickened as he searched the faces for Valerie's. With regret, he realized he couldn't expect to find her among them. He'd never seen her venture farther out the door than Annie's backyard swing set.

He looked toward the Paiges' house and glimpsed Valerie's profile at her sitting room window. Across the driveway stood an enormous cottonwood tree, which he felt sure blocked her view of the brilliant display.

"She's missing so much, all on account of fear." He lowered his head. "Valerie needs some restoring, too, Father. Show me how I can help her."

Gathering his courage, he started for the door. Then, remembering the spicy canned chili he'd heated up for supper, he made a detour to the bathroom for a quick tooth brushing and swirl of minty mouthwash. Tongue tingling, he strode downstairs and rapped loudly on the Paiges' kitchen door.

૨ત

Hearing the knock, Valerie turned from the window. She couldn't see much anyway, thanks to that tree. It completely blocked her view toward the Aileen Community Park several blocks away, where the annual fireworks show was staged.It surprised her that town officials would even hold a fireworks show this year, dry as everything was. No doubt the fire department was on high alert.

The knock sounded again. She bristled with irritation. "Doesn't Connor have his key?" As she made her way downstairs, she murmured, "Forgive me, Lord. It's myself I'm upset with, not Connor."

The sight of Healy standing on the porch, hands stuffed in his jeans pockets, sent her heart fluttering. She smoothed her hair into place before opening the door. "Hello," she said, more breathlessly than she liked. "I—we missed you at dinner. There's plenty of food left. Can I warm up a plate for you?"

He entered hesitantly. "Uh, no, thanks. I came down because I saw you were missing the fireworks."

She tried to laugh, but it sounded hollow. "Who can get excited about flashes of gunpowder? It's so noisy, and the show's over almost before it starts."

"Yeah, but you gotta admit, it's pretty impressive while it's happening."

"Really, I'm not interested." She strode to the sink, where a greasy serving platter soaked in soapy water. She drained the sink and began refilling it with fresh hot water and a generous squirt of dishwashing liquid.

A hand reached past her and shut off the faucet. She looked up into reproachful eyes. "Valerie Bishop, how long has it been since you've seen a Fourth of July fireworks show?"

"I. . .I can't remember." He stood so close that she could smell his mint-scented breath. She fought the nervous churning of her stomach.

"Then I know for a fact it's been too long." Healy took both her hands and tugged her toward the door.

"I can't go out there. Healy, please." Panic edged her voice. Healy would think she'd gone completely crazy.

"I understand you're scared, but it's okay. Trust me." Releasing one of her hands, he reached behind his back and opened the door.

Unspeakable terrors lurked beyond the reach of the porch light. Her breath quickened. She planted her feet on the doorsill.

Healy stopped and squeezed her hand. "Look at me."

At the force of his words, she settled her anxious, darting gaze on his face.

"Concentrate on my voice. Keep your eyes on me and don't think about anything else." He took a step back and pulled her one shaky step forward.

"Good," he said. "I'm here, and you're safe."

Another step. And another.

Dry grass whispered beneath her sandals. Reassuring eyes beckoned her forward. Soothing words coaxed her up the wooden stairs beside the garage, through a door beneath a yellow porch light swarming with June bugs. When Healy released his hypnotic hold, she found herself standing in the darkened living area of his apartment.

"Come look." He motioned her toward the window. "I got the best view right here."

As she neared, an exploding ball of red, white, and blue lit up the night sky. "Oh, my goodness." Breathless, she pressed her palm against the glass. "It's beautiful. I'd forgotten. . ."

Acutely aware of Healy's presence beside her, she watched in awe as one striking display after another sparkled above the treetops. It seemed an eternity and yet only moments until the sky erupted in a grand finale of color and light—pinwheels, mushrooms, chrysanthemums, and rockets. She could only murmur in wonder and delight.

The fireworks faded, leaving a thick cloud of smoke drifting across the starlit night. Below, Connor and his guests folded up their lawn chairs and returned to the house. With a sigh, she smiled up at Healy. "Thank you."

He brushed her cheek, wiping away a tear she hadn't realized had fallen. "We all have our own prisons," he said. "But sometimes the door's standing wide open and we don't even know it. And only a fool would fail to walk out that door if given the chance."

She searched his face. "What if what's outside the door is scarier than what's inside?"

"You'll never know until you step through, now, will you?" He grinned.

She couldn't help but smile back. "I suppose I just took one major step through the door tonight, thanks to you."

"You wanted to, or I'd never have been able to talk you through it." He switched on a table lamp, then ambled to the refrigerator and peered inside. "Want a soda?"

Feeling giddy, Valerie nodded. "A soda would be great."

She did want to change things, to break out of her "prison." Something about Healy made her believe for the first time that maybe she could.

eight

Valerie slipped off her sandals and tucked her feet under her skirt on the mauve tweed sofa that had once graced the living room of the Ashton Brook Lane house. Looking around the apartment, she noticed Healy had done a pretty good job of settling in. The sitting area was comfortably arranged, with the sofa facing the front windows and accented by a maple coffee table and a side table with an ivory-shaded reading lamp.

Tom's old leather recliner, a huge thing that had always swallowed Valerie, sat catty-corner to the lamp table. Sitting there now, Healy looked as relaxed as she had ever seen him. Their eyes met briefly before he lowered his gaze and grinned, obviously pleased with himself over the triumph of coaxing her upstairs to see the fireworks. And he certainly had a right to be a little smug. Healy Ferguson had achieved what no one else had managed in four years of trying.

She sipped her soft drink and smiled at him over the rim of her glass. "You're pretty proud of yourself, aren't you?"

"I'm more proud of you."

"I think I'm still in shock." She tucked a strand of hair behind her ear. "Healy Ferguson, man of many talents. I wish you'd tell me more about yourself."

"Like I said before, not much to tell." He rose stiffly and paced to the window like a nervous cat.

What secrets lay hidden behind those hooded hazel eyes? Valerie tried for a lighter tone. "Why so secretive? Are you in the witness protection program or something?"

Healy sighed and set his soda can on the windowsill. "I suppose I am keeping some things private." Staring out the window, he shoved his hands into his pockets. "I got into some trouble a number of years ago, bad trouble. I had a temper like you wouldn't believe. I—"

He paused, swallowed. "I hurt somebody. And I paid for it. And thanks to a good friend who never gave up on me, I also found forgiveness in the Lord." His voice shook. "By God's grace, I've been given a second chance."

Valerie's heart ached for him. She knew all too well the torture of reliving her own past. "I'm so sorry, Healy. About your past, and for pressuring you to talk about it. But I'm glad you had such a loyal friend."

"Wouldn't be here at all if not for him." Healy retrieved his soda can, took a long drink, and returned to the recliner.

"Do you and your friend still keep in touch?"

He looked tired. . .or was it sadness that shadowed his gaze? "He, uh. . .he died awhile back."

"Oh, Healy." Valerie scooted to the edge of the sofa and tentatively reached for his hand.

He sat forward, and his warm, calloused fingers slowly relaxed into her palm. "The really sad thing is that I never had the chance to properly thank him for all he did for me. It's the whole reason why I—" He cast Valerie a sidelong glance and abruptly withdrew his hand. "Hey, it's getting late. I should be getting you back to the house before your big brother misses you."

Valerie laughed. "Connor? Don't let him intimidate you. Besides, after what you did for me tonight, he and Ellen will be singing your praises right along with me."

"I hope you're right." He rose and helped her from the sofa. "Think you can make it on your own, or do you want me to walk with you?"

For the first time Valerie gave thought to the necessity of another trek through the darkened backyard. She pressed a hand to her roiling stomach. "Can you cast another of your spells on me?"

"I bet if you set your mind to it, you could make it just fine, but if you want, I'll stay with you all the way."

She gazed up at him with trembling lips. "I want." *Oh, Healy, I want a whole lot more than just a walk across the lawn with you!*

"All righty then." He steadied her as she took a shaky step onto the landing, then guided her slowly down the stairs.

When they arrived on the back porch, she released a grateful sigh. She gripped both his hands and squeezed them with all her might. "I made it," she said in amazement. *"I made it!"*

"Wasn't so bad after all, huh?" Healy's mouth curled into a half smile. Still clutching her hands, he leaned toward her. His lips brushed her cheek.

Her hand flew to her face. The spot where he'd kissed her seemed aflame.

Healy jerked back. He clawed stiff fingers through his hair. "I—I shouldn't have done that. For–forgive me. Guess I got caught up in the moment."

"Oh no, it's all right." She smiled shyly up at him. "It was a nice moment."

The door swung open. Ellen and Connor stood just inside the kitchen, their mouths agape.

"Thought we heard voices out here," Connor said, his brow furrowing.

Ellen grinned. "Why, Val, I thought you'd already gone upstairs to bed."

"I, uh. . ." She clasped trembling hands behind her back.

Healy cleared his throat. "I didn't want her to miss the fireworks, and I've got the best view up there." He nodded toward the apartment.

"Yes," Connor said with an appraising look, "you certainly do."

Valerie slithered past her brother. "Well, good night, Healy. Thanks again." She darted up to her room, leaving Connor and Ellen to ponder the questions she'd read in their eyes.

As she prepared for bed, she studied her reflection in the

bathroom mirror. Her cheeks glowed a little pinker than usual, her eyes brighter.

"You look like a silly schoolgirl," she chided her image in the mirror. No man had made her feel this way since she first met Tom, and after his death she'd never expected to experience these feelings again.

She closed her eyes. "Lord, where are You leading me?"

Healy. . .healing. Could they be one and the same for her?

૭

Had he really kissed her? Just a little peck on the cheek, nothing serious. . .right?

Like a zombie Healy began emptying the dish drainer, methodically placing plates and glasses in the cupboard. A knock sounded on the apartment door, and he almost dropped a coffee mug. His heart hammered. *Valerie?*

"Healy?" Connor's voice, and there was a definite edge to it.

"Uh, be right there." Had Connor seen the kiss? He gulped and pulled open the door.

The tall, blond man stepped inside, his knife-sharp stare pinning Healy to the spot. "I don't know what you did or said, but it's a downright miracle." Connor laughed aloud. "A miracle!"

Healy wrinkled his brow. He'd expected a lecture on propriety, if not a swift kick out of town. "I don't. . .understand."

"Do you know how long it took us to get Valerie to venture outside even twenty feet from the back door? And only in broad daylight. Never once since she's lived with us has she ever made it as far as the garage, much less upstairs to this apartment." Connor pressed a palm to his forehead. "Healy, how did you do it?"

He gave an embarrassed shrug. "I just talked to her, that's all. I made her focus on me, not her fears."

Connor's eyes narrowed. "That's all? After everything we've tried, you make it sound way too easy."

"Guess I've had some practice." Healy stared at the floor.

"When I was in prison, it seemed like new inmates—especially the young, scared ones—gravitated toward me. I never could forget how scared I was when they first locked me up, and I didn't want to see another kid with a lousy start in life go through that kind of terror without someone in his corner."

"Healy Ferguson, you never cease to amaze me." Connor ambled across the kitchenette and leaned his forearms on the back of the recliner. He stood there for a full minute without speaking. Then, turning slowly, he said, "Even knowing you're Tom's old friend, I had reservations about hiring an ex-con with a manslaughter conviction and letting him take up residence right upstairs from my very fragile sister." He chuckled softly. "I think of her as fragile, but she's really not. Just. . .wounded. Valerie has an inner strength the rest of us can only envy."

"She's got a deep, abiding faith in the Lord," Healy said softly. "That's where her strength comes from."

"Of course, you're right. And maybe I've been too protective of her." He sighed. "Anyway, when I realized what you'd done tonight, I had to come up and thank you."

Healy's face warmed. He shoved nervous hands into his pockets. "Just glad I could help."

ଛ

"No, I'm telling you, you'll have to come out to the garage to see." Healy stood in Valerie's sitting room. They'd been having this discussion—make that *argument*—for the past twenty minutes. But after Connor's continued encouragement to keep working on Valerie's fears, Healy wasn't about to give in.

"This is ridiculous. Why can't you bring the boards up here for me to look at?" She stomped her foot like a stubborn child, and he couldn't suppress a chuckle.

"Because," he said, rolling his eyes, "there are too many of them and it's too hot. And it's getting hotter by the minute."

"It'll be hot in the garage, too. No sense both of us getting all sweaty." She crossed her arms. "If you need my opinion so badly, bring the boards up here."

He spread his hands. "Hey, it's okay with me if you don't care how the wood grain matches up. I can build your bookshelves any old way if that's what you want."

"Ooooh, you are so stubborn."

"Me? I'm not the one standing here throwing a tantrum."

"Tantrum? Tantrum!" Valerie shook her finger in his face. "I'll give you a tantrum."

Healy burst out laughing and decided he'd never seen anyone so beautiful in his life. Her lips pushed out in a childish pout. A wisp of pale yellow hair had worked itself loose from her hair clip and hung haphazardly across one of her smoldering gray eyes.

"Healy Ferguson, stop laughing at me right this minute." With an angry huff, she swept her hair off her face. It fell right back.

"I know what you're doing." She twisted out of his reach. "I've seen you and Connor whispering, plotting. You're trying to get me away from the house again. Maybe it worked the other night, but"—she shivered—"don't push it, okay? I'm not ready to try again."

"So when will you be ready?" Healy came up behind her. It took all his resolve not to draw her into his arms.

Her voice quavered. "Maybe never."

"It's one thing to be afraid," he said, "and something else entirely to be a coward."

He waited in silence, watching her fine-boned hands clench and unclench. Her shoulders rose and fell with several deep breaths. "I know you're right, Healy, but I—"

"No buts about it. 'I can do everything through him who gives me strength.' You know that verse, don't you?"

"Philippians 4:13. I know it by heart." The fight seemed to go out of her. She turned to him and held out a shaky hand. "Okay, let's go look at some boards."

Day by day, with Healy's patience, prayers, and gentle persuasion, Valerie ventured farther and farther beyond the safety of the house and the enclosed backyard. Her heart hammered with every first step, and her breathing became so shallow that she felt sure she would die. Yet with God's help she reined in her panic and followed Healy's lead.

They began with trips outside the back gate to look at the bookshelves he was building in the garage. They counted off each painted board of the wide porch running along the front of the house, even braved the heat to sit on the white wicker rockers with glasses of iced tea and watch the cars driving by. Sometimes Maggie Jensen and red-haired little Steven from next door joined them, or Jean Franklin stopped to chat on her way to the tennis courts. The whole neighborhood, witnessing Valerie's progress, showered her with encouragement.

Finally, the first week of August, with Healy holding one hand and Annie the other, Valerie made it all the way down the front walk to the mailbox.

"Yay, Aunt Val, you did it!" Annie plucked a scarlet zinnia from the flowerbed and handed it to Valerie with a flourish.

"Thank you, sweetie." Though it was too early for the postman, she tugged open the mailbox and peered inside anyway, then happily raised and lowered the red flag several times.

"Way to go, Valerie!" She glanced across the street, where Cliff Reyna looked up from his weed pulling and gave her a thumbs-up.

She waved, then looked toward the house and shook her head. "With all the painting and landscaping Connor and Ellen have done since I've been living here, this is the first time I've seen it from this perspective." Her gaze took in the beveled Victorian porch rail, the gray siding and maroon shutters, the cupola, the brass weathervane. "Connor and Ellen have poured so much love into this home. It truly is beautiful."

"There's a whole beautiful world out here just waiting for you,"

Healy said. "It's been deprived of your presence far too long."

A car roared past. Valerie cried out and fell into Healy's open arms, burying her face against his rock-solid chest. He held her until the terror subsided, then guided her toward the porch while Annie protectively clutched her other hand. She clambered toward the door, but Healy stopped her.

"No," he said, leading her to one of the wicker chairs, "you're going to stay out here and beat this fear. You're going to see that everything's all right."

"Healy, I can't. Please—" Memories of another car on a dark, rain-slicked street seized her heart, sending it racing all over again.

Healy pressed her backward until she had no choice but to sit down. "Breathe," he commanded her. "Take it in. . .let it out."

She closed her eyes and obeyed.

"It was just a silly old car," Annie said, stroking Valerie's arm. "There now, no reason to be all a-scared."

"Out of the mouths of babes." Valerie glanced at her niece with a grateful smile.

The pounding in her chest subsided. The terrifying shadows at the edge of her mind withdrew.

"Thanks, sweetie. I think I'm going to be okay." She looked up into Healy's tender gaze, and she actually believed it.

%

Pastor Henke sat across from her in the living room the following Sunday afternoon. "Valerie, I'm so proud of you. At this rate, I expect to see you in church any Sunday now."

"Nothing would mean more to me." She fingered the crocheted edging of a throw pillow. "But the mere thought of getting in the car and actually driving somewhere still sends shivers up my spine."

Pastor Henke nibbled on a slice of banana bread Ellen had baked yesterday. "From the very start, I had such an extraordinary sense that Healy was sent here by God. And just as

I thought, he was meant to do far more than painting and carpentry."

Valerie absently twisted her wedding band. She could hear Connor and Ellen's muted laughter as they watched an animated video with Annie in the den. "Pastor, Tom's been gone almost five years now. Am I being foolish? I mean, do you think it's possible. . ."

A shadow crossed his face. "Are you becoming interested in Healy as more than a handyman and friend?"

"Yes, I think I am." She bit her lip. "It feels right somehow, and yet when I think of Tom and all we shared. . .and all we lost. . ."

The pastor rubbed his hands along the arms of the beige brocade chair. "Healy has lost a great deal, too," he said slowly. "He's a good man, and worthy of your affection, but tread carefully, my dear."

She studied his expression. "Why do I get the feeling you're keeping something from me? And Connor, too. You both know more about Healy's past than you're letting on." Her insides clenched. She pressed a hand to her forehead. "I get so tired of people walking on eggshells around me."

"If it seems that way, my dear, it is only because we all care about you so much."

"But I'm getting stronger, and I think I'm entitled to know the truth." She sent up a prayer before blurting out the question plaguing her heart. "Pastor, Healy has already told me about his temper getting him into trouble. Is there any reason to think he might be. . .dangerous?"

"Oh no," the pastor answered quickly. "Healy is a changed man. He would never physically hurt you or anyone else—of that I'm entirely confident."

She sat forward, her confusion deepening. "Then why do I get the impression you're warning me not to let myself become involved with him?"

Pastor Henke released a gentle laugh. "I'm a crusty old

widower. I would never presume to give anyone advice about matters of the heart."

She couldn't suppress a laugh of her own. "Since when have you ever been short on advice about any topic? Please, Pastor." She grew serious again. "If there's something I should know, then tell me."

"Trust your heart, my dear. It will tell you all you need to know for now."

She looked away and trembled. "I don't know if I dare trust my own heart in this situation."

"But you can trust the Holy Spirit. Don't be afraid of where God leads you." Pastor Henke touched her arm. "In the meantime, my only advice is to take plenty of time to get to know Healy. . .and to let him get to know you."

His cryptic words only added fuel to her mounting frustration. "Won't you give me even a small clue about his past, something that might help me understand him better?"

"Better he tells you himself, when the time is right. . .for both of you."

Valerie rose and crossed to the window. Heat shimmered off the pavement as the August sun beat mercilessly down. "But if everything you've hinted at so far is true, then Healy and I have both wasted too much time already."

We all have our own prisons, he had told her after the fireworks ended that night.

She spun around and locked her gaze upon the pastor. "Healy's been in prison, hasn't he?"

nine

"You're awful quiet today." Healy chewed the inside of his cheek as he positioned a glass-front door on Valerie's new built-in curio cabinet. "Matter of fact, you've been quiet all week."

Valerie handed him a pencil, and he marked the screw holes for the hinges. "I've been doing a lot of thinking."

His stomach did a flip-flop. Second thoughts about him, he imagined. Fearing Connor's wrath, he'd never let himself come even close to kissing her again, not even a chaste peck on the cheek, since the Fourth of July.

But, oh, how he'd wanted to. Had she sensed it? More than once he'd prayed about his growing feelings for his best friend's widow. But how could she—how could anyone—love a man who'd served time for killing someone?

So what if he'd accepted Christ, repented, paid his debt to society? He had no education beyond his prison vocational classes and a GED. When he walked out the prison gate a year ago, he'd started his new life with nothing but Tom's Bible, a couple changes of clothes, and the little money he'd saved. No woman in her right mind would even consider a relationship with a loser like him.

True, Valerie didn't know about the prison part yet, but from the moment he showed up at her front door in castoff clothing from Zion Community Church's donation barrel, the rest had to be obvious. She was way too good for him, and she must have finally started to realize it. Nothing else could explain her recent coolness.

He reached for the electric drill to make his pilot holes. Valerie supported the door as he secured the satin-finish hinges with matching brass screws. They repeated the process for the opposite door.

"It looks beautiful," Valerie said, stepping back. "Healy, you're a fine carpenter."

He murmured his thanks and raked a hand through his sweat-dampened hair. "One more set of doors and it'll be finished."

She sighed. "And on to Connor and Ellen's next project. Probably the new baby's nursery."

Did he only imagine a wistful tone in her voice?

She pressed a hand to her back and crossed to the delicate-looking antique desk. He'd noticed her writing in a book there a few times while he worked but sensed she preferred to keep the contents private.

Kind of like him and prison.

"Looks like a good time to break for a cold drink." He started for the hallway.

"Healy, wait." She turned toward him.

His heart thudded. "Yeah?"

"A few days ago Pastor Henke admitted to me what he and Connor have known about you from the beginning." He saw pity in her eyes, a look he'd never wanted to receive from a woman he cared so much about. "Healy. . .I know you've been in prison."

Thank the Lord little Annie had already gone down for her nap. He rubbed his jaw. Okay, so Valerie knew the truth now, at least that part of it. "I sure didn't mean to deceive you. It's just that the pastor and your brother thought—"

"I understand." She reached out, almost touched him, but drew back at the last moment. "I know they were. . ." She bit her lip. "They were concerned about my reaction because of what happened to my husband."

"Tom." He hung his head.

"Yes. His death and everything surrounding it has haunted me all these years." She stared at the floor. "You've helped me so much with my panic attacks when no one else seemed able to. But when I found out you had. . .you were. . ."

"Sent to jail for manslaughter," he supplied throatily.

She lifted her gaze to meet his. "It came as a shock, just when I felt we were getting to know each other. I knew you must have been through some rough times, but I had no idea. I wasn't prepared for the truth."

He tried to laugh. "Hard to ever be prepared to learn that kind of truth about somebody." He thought of Tom and the look of shock and utter despair in his eyes when he came to see Healy in jail the day after his arrest.

"What I'm trying to say," Valerie continued, "is that I should have come to you right away. You're a good man, Healy. A godly man. How could I doubt for an instant that you are a different person from who you were so many years ago?"

She reached out again, and this time her touch shot tingling currents of electricity through him. "Healy, will you tell me. . . in your own words. . .what happened?"

❧

She pulled him over to the loveseat and sat next to him without releasing his hand. His palm felt cold and damp. She longed to wrap her arms around him and take away the fear, just as he had helped her confront her own private terrors.

"I was seventeen," he began, his voice low and tremulous. "My sister had been dating this older guy. I'd seen bruises and suspected he slapped her around, but she always denied it. She seemed so hungry to be loved."

Valerie squeezed his hand. "I can't imagine any woman needing love so much that she'd willingly put up with such treatment."

Healy made a harsh noise in his throat. "Guess she didn't know any better. When we were little, our dad got killed in a construction accident, and Mama had to work long hours to provide for us. Years later, she got sick and died. Bethy, my sister, was fifteen, and I'd just turned twelve. We went to live with an aunt."

He clasped his hands between his knees. "Bethy dropped out of school and started hanging with a rough crowd, doing all sorts of things our mama had tried to teach us not to do. She did her best to raise us right, got us to Sunday school and all, but it was hard to believe in a God who'd let such horrible things happen to a good woman."

Valerie nodded. "I went through a time when I asked similar questions, myself."

"I'm not saying all this to excuse myself, but maybe it helps you see where I got off track. I lived on anger back then, but I made it to my senior year without much more trouble than occasional suspension for giving somebody a black eye or broken nose." He gave a cheerless laugh. "My temper actually gave me an edge on the football field."

"You played football?" Valerie gave him a half smile. "My Tom played in high school, too. He used to say it helped him burn off his raging teenage hormones."

Healy cast her an unreadable look before glancing away. "Teenage hormones can't be blamed for what I did. When I saw that guy hitting my sister one night, I knew real anger, real hatred, for the very first time." His whole body trembled. "I heard his car pull into the driveway near midnight. He was drunk and yelling for Bethy. He accused her of being with another guy and carried on about how he'd beat the tar out of them both."

"Oh, Healy."

He went on as if she weren't even there. "I tried to stop her, but she told me it would be okay. She thought she could talk some sense into him before he woke the whole neighborhood. Then he grabbed her arm and slapped her over and over again. Her mouth was bleeding, and she kept whimpering, begging him to stop, and suddenly I couldn't take it anymore. I ran out and started punching him. He fell backwards and hit his head on the concrete." He let out a shuddering breath. "He never got up."

A hush descended around them in the sun-brightened sitting room. Slowly, with immense tenderness, Valerie drew him into her arms and held him. She stroked his dark blond hair and breathed in the masculine smells of wood stain, sawdust, and sweat as he emptied himself of tears against her shoulder.

"It's all right, Healy," she whispered. "It's all in the past now. It's over." *And I love you.*

&

Valerie, I'm falling in love with you. He wanted so badly to say the words aloud to the woman who had finally pierced the armor around his heart.

He pulled away with a sniff. "Sorry, didn't mean to lose it like that." He grabbed some tissues and blew his nose. "Just when I think I've gotten past it, the disgusting truth jars me back to reality. No two ways about it, I'm a murderer."

"But you were defending your sister. Didn't the courts take that into consideration?"

Methodically he folded the damp tissues. Their baby powder smell lingered in his nostrils, playing sweet counterpoint to the bitter memories. "Oh sure, until they heard testimony from my high school principal, counselor, and a couple of football coaches whose players I sent to the hospital after some post-game brawls."

"But surely that wasn't enough—"

"It gets worse." He hauled in a long, shaky breath. "The coroner testified I hit the guy so many times that he was probably already unconscious when he fell."

She rose and crossed the room, then spun around to face him, an explosive fire brightening her eyes. "I don't care what they said about you in court. Healy, you've paid the penalty for your crime. And just like the Bible says, you're now a new creation in Christ. When I look at you today, I see a good, honest, decent man. I see a man of immense talent and skill."

She ran a finger along the cabinet door, and her voice grew

hoarse with emotion. "The past is behind you. You have a wonderful future ahead. Oh, Healy, I just know it."

"If you're going to give me the God-isn't-finished-with-you-yet speech, you don't have to. If I didn't already believe He has a better plan for my life, I wouldn't have made it this far."

He should tell her about Tom now. She should know the part her husband had played in Healy's redemption. "Valerie, there's something else—"

"Hey, Aunt Val." Annie sauntered into the room, dragging an oversized stuffed rabbit. "I woke up from my nap and I want my snack now."

"Hi, sweetie. Did you sleep good?" Valerie gave Healy a regretful look that told him they'd have to put their conversation on hold for a little while. "Come on downstairs, and we'll see what kind of cookies we can find."

"Healy, you come, too." Annie reached for his hand.

As he grasped her pudgy pink fist and allowed himself to be dragged downstairs, he indulged in a few pleasurable moments of fantasizing—Valerie, himself, a kid or two of their own. With steady carpentry work maybe he could someday afford a nice little house for his family. Jesus had been a carpenter, after all. It was honest, respectable work, and Healy knew he was good at it.

Maybe it was a gift from God that he'd been stopped from telling Valerie about his connection to Tom. At least this way, whatever she felt for Healy, he could be sure it wasn't clouded by any sense of obligation or pity toward her deceased husband's old buddy from prison.

So he'd wait—wait to tell her that part until he got the okay from Connor or Pastor Henke. . .or from the Lord.

And, Lord, if I'm not supposed to be falling in love with her, You'd better stop me quick, because I'm falling hard and fast.

ten

Valerie peered around the corner of the open garage door and stood watching Healy. Sweat gleamed on his tanned, muscular arms as he measured and marked a piece of lumber for the new sink cabinet for the upstairs guest bathroom.

Smiling, she crept up from behind and snaked her arm around him until the booklet she held was right in front of his face.

"What in the world—" He grabbed it out of her hands with feigned annoyance. "Can't a guy get any work done around here without some pretty lady pestering him?"

"Pretty lady, is it?" Her heart thrilled. "When the guy is as handsome and talented as you are, what do you expect?"

Color rose in Healy's face. He hid it behind the booklet he'd wrenched from her grasp. "All right, let's see what you found so important that you had to come all the way out here and interrupt my work."

Fizzy as a shaken-up pop bottle, she blurted out the answer. "It's a course catalogue from East Central College. I asked Ellen to bring one home with her yesterday."

"College?" Healy held the catalogue away from him as if it were on fire.

"There's still time to register for the fall, and they offer business and vocational courses, and I thought—"

She cut herself off at the terrified look in Healy's eyes. "I—I thought going back to school might be another positive step toward your new start in life."

He edged away and slowly turned the pages. His Adam's apple quivered. "I used to dream about going to college. . . ."

"Well, here's your chance." Urgency filled her. She fixed

him with a determined stare. "Healy, you can do it. You can do anything you set your mind to."

He rubbed the back of his neck with a dirty hand. "You're forgetting I don't have a car, or even a driver's license. How would I get there?"

"If you can plan your class schedule to match Ellen's, you can ride with her. If not, something else will work out."

He looked askance at her. "You seem awful sure of yourself."

"Hey, aren't you the guy who's been quoting Philippians 4:13 all summer?"

"Okay, but you're forgetting one major detail. Even with what Connor pays me, I haven't saved near enough for college."

Valerie set her hands on her hips. "Healy Ferguson, for a man of faith, sometimes you sure don't show much. You happen to be looking at the church prayer-chain coordinator, remember? The calls have already been made. People are praying as we speak."

His mouth spread into a broad grin, and his hazel eyes lit up. "You are truly the most amazing woman I have ever known." Then he let loose a whoop of victory. He swept Valerie into his arms and whirled her around the hot, stuffy garage. "Hey, world, I'm gonna be a college man!"

"Healy, oh, Healy!" Laughing, she wrapped her arms around his neck. Her head still spun when he finally set her down. She pressed a hand to her lower back but smiled in spite of the nagging ache.

Worry filled Healy's eyes. "Did I hurt you? Are you okay?"

"I'm fine. I'm just so happy to see you this excited."

He held her at arm's length. "Valerie, I. . ." His throat worked, and he seemed to want to tell her something but couldn't get the words out.

Say it, Healy. Say you love me.

Lowering his eyes, he murmured, "I can't believe how lucky—no, how *blessed* I am to have found you. Nobody has believed in me like you have since—"

"Oh, hush." She silenced him with a finger to his lips. She looked up at him coyly, surprising herself with the sudden yearning she felt. "If you really think I'm so amazing, then why don't you kiss me?"

Kiss her?

He didn't need to be asked twice. He drew her to him, so close that he could smell the delicate honeysuckle scent of her shampoo. His lips hovered over hers for the briefest of moments before he gently, tenderly kissed her. The warmth of her mouth made his head swim. He relished an ecstasy he never imagined possible. No wonder Tom had fallen helplessly, head-over-heels in love with this woman.

He drew back, and for a moment her lips seemed to follow his. He sensed in her the same keen urgency welling up in himself.

"Valerie, oh, Valerie!" He gave a ragged sigh. "Tell me I'm crazy, tell me it's hopeless, but I'm in love with you. I think I have been since the first minute I laid eyes on you."

"You're not crazy," she said, her voice like liquid silver. "I'm falling in love with you, too."

Resisting every urge churning inside him, he pushed her away. His pulse throbbed in his ears. "You'd better go inside. It's safer. . .for both of us."

Her honeyed laugh floated in the sultry air. "Sorry, Healy, but as hard as you fought to get me through that locked door, you're going to find it a lot harder to banish me to the house again."

He couldn't help but grin despite the doubts coiling around his heart. She was so incredibly beautiful. And stubborn as they came. "I just meant that we should both slow down here. You haven't known me very long, and with what you do know, you ought to be at least a little cautious, don't you think?"

A shivery sigh escaped her lips. "I'm not afraid of your past or of who you used to be. But you're right, we should take things slowly." She ran a slender finger along the jagged white scar on his left forearm. "We're both scarred from old wounds, and we need to make sure we're fully healed."

Sadness crept into her eyes. Every time Healy thought about how Tom died, it made his stomach wrench. The pain must be a million times worse for Valerie. She saw it happen. She watched her husband's blood drain away in a senseless, pointless act of carnage.

"Hey, seriously, it's the hottest part of the afternoon." He covered the catch in his voice with a cough. "You should go inside. We can talk more about. . .us. . .later."

"Will you join us for supper?"

He chewed his lip. "Okay, as long as you and Ellen and Connor don't gang up on me about this college stuff."

"But you will think about it, won't you?"

"Count on it." He brought the catalogue to his forehead in a mock salute before stuffing it into his back pocket. "Now get out of here so I can finish up."

&

As Valerie sauntered toward the house, she could still taste the delightful warmth of Healy's lips and feel his rock-hard arms around her.

O Lord, I know my feelings for Healy are real, but I'm scared.

Not like the paralyzing fear of her panic attacks, but the fear of falling deeply, hopelessly in love with this man and then losing him. Losing him the way she lost Tom. Maybe not to a violent act of crime, but what about a car accident, or a hair dryer falling into the bathtub with him? Or alone in the garage he could injure himself with one of those noisy power tools and bleed to death before anyone found him.

"Perfect love casts out fear. Cast all your worries on Me."

"I know, Father." She glanced toward the cloudless blue sky. "I'm trying. Help me, as only You can."

As she bent down to pick up one of Annie's toys, another searing pain shot through her back. She gasped and doubled over, bracing her hands on her knees, and silently acknowledged one more reason she could lose Healy.

She'd have to tell him. Soon.

The back door opened. "Val, are you okay?" Ellen hurried down the porch steps and helped Valerie inside.

"I'll be all right in a minute. Just let me sit down and rest." She eased into the nearest kitchen chair.

"Turn around. I'll rub it for you." Ellen pressed firm hands against the painful spot on Valerie's back, kneading the soreness away.

"Thanks. That feels great." She rested her head on the table and relaxed into her sister-in-law's massage.

"How's Healy coming with the bathroom cabinet?"

Valerie gave a soft chuckle in spite of her discomfort. "We didn't talk much about the cabinet."

"Hmmm. Okay, what did you talk about? You were out there long enough." Ellen gave Valerie's back a final brisk rub and plopped down in the chair across from her.

Sitting up, Valerie smoothed her hair away from her face. "I showed him the college catalogue."

"And?"

"It might take some doing, but I think he can be convinced."

Ellen sipped the cranberry juice she'd left sitting on the table. "I'll be happy to help him register and show him around campus. He'll have to go through some testing, but maybe I can pull a few strings to smooth the process for him." She winked. "But I have a feeling you and your prayer chain will soon have the entire situation under control."

"I really appreciate how accepting of him you and Connor have been." Valerie reached across the table to squeeze Ellen's hand.

"I admit, I was stunned when Connor finally told me about Healy's time in prison. I can't believe he and Pastor Henke kept it between themselves for so long." She grimaced. "Well, yes, I can."

Valerie shot her sister-in-law a wry grin. "Right. What is it

Connor always says? 'Telephone, telegraph, tell Ellen.'"

"Ugh, don't rub it in." Ellen went to the stove to stir a pot of marinara sauce. The garlic-and-tomato aroma filled the kitchen.

"Anyway," Valerie continued, "you can see what a good man Healy is. That part of his life was so long ago, and he paid for his mistake."

Ellen smiled over her shoulder. "You're falling fast, aren't you?"

"Am I so obvious?"

"Like a neon sign." Ellen laid aside the wooden spoon. "Valerie Bishop is"—she flashed the quotation marks symbol with the first two fingers of each hand—"*in love.*"

Valerie cast her a pleading look. "What am I going to do? One minute I'm sure it's so right, and the next, I'm quaking in my sandals."

Tenderness softened Ellen's voice. "Honey, you've been in love before, and you know how it works. You take it one day at a time. And if Healy is the man God wants you to be with, He'll take care of the details."

"I'm not being a traitor to Tom's memory, am I?"

"Of course not. And I think you already knew the answer to that question. Come on, what's really bothering you?" She dropped several handfuls of bowtie pasta into a pot of boiling water. "Are you more hung up on Healy's past than you can admit to yourself?"

Valerie rose and stretched, then went to the cupboard and took out a stack of dinner plates. "It threw me for a loop at first, but all I have to do is spend ten minutes with him and I know what a wonderful man he is."

"Then what's the problem?"

The back door swung open and Connor breezed in. "Mmm, Italian. My favorite." He planted a noisy kiss on Ellen's cheek.

"Come back here," she demanded when he turned away. "You can do better than that." Grabbing a chunk of his blond hair, she pulled his face to hers and kissed him passionately.

The color rose in his face as Ellen released him. "It's the marinara sauce," he said, winking at Valerie. "Always does that to her. You know, Italian, the food of romance?"

"Oh, and I thought it was the bloom of pregnancy." Valerie raised an eyebrow as she busied herself arranging flatware.

"Well, romance is in the air," Ellen said brightly.

Valerie looked up at a light tapping on the back door. Connor strode over to answer it. "Hey, Healy, come on in."

He looked scrubbed and fresh from the shower, his wet hair slicked back and dark blond curls brushing the collar of a pale blue polo shirt. "Am I too early? Valerie invited me for supper."

Connor clamped a hand on Healy's shoulder. In a loud stage whisper he said, "We're having Italian. Enter at your own risk."

At Healy's questioning look, Valerie could only shrug. *Lord, if You're going to let Connor and Ellen play matchmaker, I'll need an extra dose of Your courage.*

eleven

Healy settled into the passenger seat of Ellen's blue Mazda, then looked up at Valerie. "I wish you'd come with me."

She wanted to, more than she could ever tell him, but her heart still raced at the mere thought of venturing far from the familiarity of home. She shook her head and gently closed his door, forcing her thoughts toward the surprise she planned for Healy when he returned. Bending toward his open window, she said, "I'll stay here and pray for you the whole time you're gone."

Ellen laughed and climbed in behind the steering wheel. "We're only going to get him registered for school, Val. You make it sound like he's headed to death row." She threw her hand over her mouth. "Oh, Healy, I'm so sorry. I wasn't thinking."

"If I'm not used to prison jokes by now, I never will be." He blew a limp strand of hair off his damp forehead and grinned at Ellen. "What do you say we get this show on the road before I chicken out or we both melt from the heat, whichever comes first?"

Ellen started the car and turned the air conditioner on full blast. She leaned over the steering wheel and gave Valerie a thumbs-up. "If all goes well, we should be back by six."

Valerie tilted her head to give Healy a quick kiss. "I'm so glad you're doing this." She waved as they backed out of the driveway.

ðû

Ellen flipped on her signal and turned at the next corner. "You don't have to look so scared, you know."

"Can't help it. This college thing is almost as scary as prison ever was. I don't know if I can cut it." He could feel himself breaking into a cold sweat despite the frigid air blowing in his face.

Ellen tossed a smile in his direction. "Val has every confidence in you. I know you'll make her proud."

"I'd like to do more than make her proud." He rubbed his brow. "I'd like to. . ."

"I know you're falling for her." Ellen spoke slowly as she stared at the road ahead. "Be careful, Healy. She's a strong, determined woman, but she still has some healing to do."

"Believe me, I'm not rushing into anything. Besides, what do I have to offer someone like her?" The old feelings of worthlessness welled inside him. "She deserves so much more, someone who can give her a real home, someone who can provide for her the way she deserves." *Someone without a past.*

"Love doesn't usually take those details into consideration," Ellen replied. "It just happens."

"Still, I can't even let myself dream about a future with Valerie unless I know I could give her a decent life. She's already been married to the best and most upright guy who ever walked the face of the earth." He stared forlornly at the passing countryside. "Why she even gives me the time of day, I'll never understand."

Ellen cast him a quizzical glance. "You almost talk as if you knew Tom."

His stomach knotted. "I did."

By the time Ellen parked her car in the faculty lot, Healy had told her everything about his connection with Tom and how the search for his friend had brought him to St. Louis and finally Aileen.

She cut off the engine and drummed her fingers on the steering wheel. "I am going to have a serious talk with my husband later. Is there anything *else* he and Pastor Henke have neglected to tell me about you?"

Healy ducked his head. "That about covers it. After Valerie

guessed I'd been in prison, I thought maybe Connor would go ahead and tell her about me and Tom. I even asked him about it a couple times, but he said we had to take it one step at a time, said he still has hopes of getting her back into counseling before we lay too much more on her."

"I suppose that makes sense. But still. . .I can't believe Valerie hasn't put the pieces together for herself. Why, even I remember Tom mentioning his correspondence with a friend in prison."

Healy rubbed perspiring hands on his thighs. "When I think about how Tom died, all she went through herself—it's no wonder she can't remember some things."

Ellen gave her brown curls a rapid toss as she reached into the back seat for her purse. "And you, Healy, losing your best friend. . . I'm so sorry."

"Tom was too good a man to suffer that way." With a ragged sigh, Healy shoved his door open and stepped into the August heat.

Coming around the car, Ellen touched his arm. "It seems to me you have two people to make proud with this decision to go to college. Tom holds as much a stake in your future as Valerie does."

Healy stared across the sloping lawns toward the rambling brick buildings. "And I owe him. I owe him big-time."

❧

Valerie hummed along with a Christian radio station while she put the finishing touches on a banner she'd been creating on the computer:

FOR WISDOM WILL ENTER YOUR HEART, AND KNOWLEDGE
WILL BE PLEASANT TO YOUR SOUL.
—PROVERBS 2:10
CONGRATULATIONS ON YOUR EXCITING NEW BEGINNING!

While bright yellow paper slowly fed through the color

printer, she went to check on a sheet of cookies in the oven. The tempting aroma of melting chocolate chips swirled around her. Unable to wait a second longer, she dipped a spoon into the tub of pre-mixed cookie dough and scooped out a gooey, delicious mouthful.

She was still savoring the chocolaty sweetness when the phone rang a few moments later.

"Good afternoon, Valerie. How's my favorite prayer-chain coordinator?"

"Hi, Pastor! Couldn't be better. You sound as if you have an assignment for me." She took one last lick from the spoon.

"In fact, I do." Pastor Henke sighed softly. "You're familiar with the Sanderson family."

Valerie had met the Sandersons once when she and Tom visited Zion, and she'd read about the family often in the church newsletter since coming to live with her brother. Harold Sanderson owned a prominent investment company and held the reputation of being one of Zion's biggest financial contributors. However, both Connor and Ellen had hinted on more than one occasion that Harold had a tendency to throw his weight around until he got things done his way.

But Harold's money had not been able to ensure a trouble-free family life. Seemed as if one or another of his four spoiled children was always getting into mischief—drinking binges, speeding tickets, vandalizing the high school, truancy. The older ones had somehow managed to grow up, shape up, and move out on their own. That left only the Sandersons' teenage daughter. Valerie chewed her lip. "Oh no, what's Marsha done this time?"

"She and a friend were in a car accident last night. Marsha wasn't seriously injured, praise God, but her friend Tina Maxwell has a broken rib and a mild concussion."

"Oh dear. Is there no end to trouble for that family?"

"I'm afraid it gets worse. Marsha's accident occurred after she and Tina were caught shoplifting." Pastor Henke paused, cleared his throat. "Seems they were trying to make a quick getaway."

She pressed a hand to her stomach and mentally pushed away a disturbing memory. "Have charges been filed?"

"For Tina, yes. Marsha was taken into custody but, as always, Harold's attorney pulled some strings and got her charges dropped." His crisp tone left no doubt concerning his opinion of such tactics.

The oven timer chimed. Valerie removed the sheet of cookies while balancing the phone against her shoulder. "Somebody needs to talk to the Sandersons about tough love."

"I assure you, I have tried." Pastor Henke huffed. "At any rate, would you please activate the prayer chain for Tina? Her family doesn't attend Zion. In fact, I'm not sure they're Christians at all, but all the more reason why she needs prayer. And, of course, add the Sandersons to the list. . .for obvious reasons."

"I certainly will." Valerie jotted a note on the tablet by the phone.

"Moving on to a more pleasant topic," Pastor Henke began, "did you get our budding new student off to matriculate?"

Valerie's heart lightened. "Ellen should be walking him through the registration process as we speak." She tacked the prayer reminder on the bulletin board next to her list of emergency phone numbers. "I'm so excited for him. He deserves this chance for a better life."

"I'm still planning to be there for his celebratory dinner. Six thirty, right?"

"Bring your appetite. Connor's going to throw some salmon steaks on the grill, and, of course, Ellen has lots of fixings already prepared. I'm in charge of dessert."

Silence met her ears. Then she heard a tentative, "You. . .made dessert?"

"Oh, please. You sound as if you don't think I'm capable."

"Er, well, I do recall the pumpkin pie you attempted a

couple of Thanksgivings ago."

She pursed her lips. "I can't help it if I never made pie from a real pumpkin before. How was I supposed to know to remove the seeds first?" She laughed. "Anyway, you don't have to worry. Everything is store-bought, from the pre-mixed cookie dough to the old-fashioned vanilla ice cream."

"Whew, I am utterly relieved."

"I'd better go, Pastor." Valerie dropped her spoon into soapy dishwater. "I'd like to get those prayer-chain calls made before Annie wakes up from her nap. She's going to help me decorate Healy's apartment while he's out."

They said their good-byes, and Valerie reached in the drawer for her prayer-chain phone list. The calls went quickly—no one seemed to require much explanation about another Sanderson sibling in trouble.

As she hung up from the last conversation, Annie skipped into the kitchen. The curly-haired child sniffed the air and broke into a grin. "I smell cookies, Aunt Val."

"You sure do, sweetie." Valerie swiftly moved the tray of cooling cookies out of Annie's reach. "But we have to save these for later."

"Healy's party. Yay!"

Valerie whisked the container of dough into the refrigerator. "Come on, Annie-girl, let's go decorate. Afterward, I'll let you have one cookie with a glass of milk."

Already perspiring as she unlocked Healy's door, she mentally thanked him for leaving the air conditioner running. She set her armload of decorating supplies on the kitchen table and surveyed the room. Her mouth curled into an approving smile. "My goodness, this place is neat as a pin. You'd never guess a bachelor lived here." Ever since he'd been working on Connor's house, Valerie had observed Healy's meticulous care of everything, from the professional power tools Connor had rented to the tiniest paintbrush. She admired and respected Healy more every day.

"Put the banner right there." Annie pointed to the wide archway between the dining area and living room.

"Good idea." Valerie positioned a chair and climbed up carefully, ever conscious of the twinge in her lower back.

With the banner hung to her satisfaction, she carried a package of balloons to the sofa and sat down to start inflating them. After blowing up the first three, she felt a twinge of lightheadedness and leaned back to catch her breath. She could hardly restrain her laughter as Annie took up the project, puffing and spitting but making little headway with the stiff, stubborn balloon.

Suddenly the balloon shot out of Annie's mouth and landed on an end table. She scurried over to retrieve it. "Hey, Aunt Val, Healy has a big Bible like Daddy's. I wonder if his has pictures, too." She tossed the balloon aside and began paging through the black leather-bound book.

"Oh, Annie, be careful." Valerie reached to rescue Healy's Bible. "You don't want to tear the pages. Healy wouldn't like—"

The Bible fell open in her lap, revealing the flyleaf. As she glanced down, the sight of familiar handwriting wrenched her heart.

To Gus, my best friend. . .

Shock and disbelief sent chills up her arms. *"Tom?"*

Memories long submerged flooded her consciousness. Gus, Tom's high-school football buddy from his hometown in Michigan, the kid who had accidentally killed someone in a fight and ended up going to prison. How many times had Tom talked about visiting his friend at the state penitentiary, giving him a Bible, helping him find forgiveness in Christ? Though Tom never got back to Michigan, he faithfully wrote to his friend, sometimes as often as once a week.

Including the day he died.

"I'll be ready to leave in a minute, Lady V."

The chasm of the past four years was bridged in a moment,

and she could hear Tom's tired but cheery voice as clearly as she did that night.

"I know it's late, but I just want to finish this letter to Gus. We can drop it in the corner mailbox on the way home."

She remembered leaning in the office doorway, feeling so sleepy that she could scarcely keep her eyes open. The aromas of olive oil, Italian sausage, and pungent spices still lingered in the air. Commingled with the sharp odor of disinfectant cleaner, the smells conspired to nauseate her.

"Good night, Pablo. See you tomorrow, Manny," she called to the busboys, yawning as she followed them to the back door to lock it behind them. With each step, the boys' rubber-soled shoes squeaked on the tile floor, still wet from the last mopping of the day.

Returning to the office, she watched Tom seal the envelope and peel a stamp from the roll in his desk drawer. He gave her an apologetic smile as he rose and slipped his arms into his jacket. "Is my little Italian mama about to fall asleep standing up?"

"I'm Irish, not Italian, and yes." She leaned into the comfort of his embrace.

Tom held the front door open for her, and the October evening met them with a cold, misting rain. Across the street, the U.S. mailbox shimmered under a haloed streetlight.

"Wait here. I'll be right back." Tom sprinted across the slick pavement, letter in hand.

She stood in the shelter of the green awning over the door, hands stuffed into the fleece-lined pockets of her coat. A few blocks away, a police siren wailed. It seemed to be moving closer. Tom waved and started back across the street.

Suddenly tires screeched. Headlights blinded her. A sickening thud and a woman's scream—her own. A car spun out of control. Metal slammed against metal. Glass shattered.

A stranger's face filled her vision. A rough hand clamped around her arm; another covered her mouth. She tasted sweat and fear. A dangerous, hate-filled voice shouted in her ear, "Lady, you're coming with me, or I'll kill you right here!"

Dear God, help me. Tom, get up, get up—please!

The police sirens were upon them now, splintering the night air. Blue and red strobes sliced through the mist and reflected in her captor's wide, panicked eyes. Blood oozed from a gash on his temple, crisscrossing an angry scar across his left cheek.

"Let the lady go," someone shouted. "Don't make things worse than they already are."

He made an ugly noise in his throat—half terror, half rage—before thrusting her hard against something metal, something sharp. Pain shot through her back, and she screamed. With one hand she groped for something to brace against; with the other she cradled her abdomen. She raised her head as her assailant and the two men with him plunged into the night, police in pursuit.

And then blessed blackness.

twelve

"Aunt Val? Aunt Val, why are you crying?" Annie's shrill, frightened pleas slowly penetrated the fog of Valerie's mind.

"I'll be all right, honey. Just. . .give me a minute." Dazed, emptied, she barely recognized the sound of her own voice, taut and thin as an overstretched rubber band.

As long suppressed memories converged with reality, the unspeakable truth jolted her with brutal force. If Tom had not crossed the street, if he hadn't chosen that moment to mail the letter to Gus. . .to *H. P. Ferguson, Prisoner #6397104*. . .he would still be alive.

It seemed impossible, and yet the evidence lay before her in Tom's own handwriting in the front of Healy's Bible, the one Healy told her his best friend had given him fifteen years ago.

How could she not have known? Hadn't she carried Tom's letters to the mailbox on many occasions? Tom had always called his friend Gus, but why hadn't she at least recognized the last name? If nothing else, she might have pieced things together listening to Healy describe the fight that sent him to prison. *Defending his sister. . .got carried away. . .*weren't those the words Tom had used when he first told her about his friend in prison?

You didn't remember because you didn't want to. You couldn't bear the pain of remembering.

The truth pressed on her heart like a crushing weight. How could she ever look at Healy the same way again?

O God, why? I loved him so!

With trembling hands she returned the Bible to the end table. "Let's go, Annie."

"But the balloons. And the streamers." Annie tugged on

Valerie's wrist. "Aren't we gonna decorate?"

"We have to go now, Annie." She staggered out into the oppressive heat.

Reaching the house, she closed the kitchen door and mechanically punched in the code to arm the security system, which, with strange detachment, she realized she had not felt the compulsion to do in weeks.

§

"Here you go, Mr. Ferguson." The gray-haired woman behind the counter slid a stack of computer printouts across to Healy. "Your class schedule and receipts. The bookstore is open if you'd like to purchase your textbooks."

Ellen touched Healy's arm. "Valerie's probably bitten her nails to the quick by now. We can get your books another day."

Healy chuckled. "After handing over so much money for tuition and fees, I could use a few days to recover from the shock before laying out another small fortune on textbooks."

"Getting an education is not cheap," Ellen said as they headed toward the parking lot. "But the grant information Mrs. Kelsey gave you should help, at least for next semester."

He shook his head. "I still can't get over the idea of total strangers from your church offering to cover my expenses to get me started. I don't know how I'll ever repay them—or you and Connor for all you've done."

Ellen aimed the key-chain remote at her shiny blue car and punched a button. "Get it through your head once and for all, Healy Ferguson. This is not about payback. It's about accepting help when you need it."

"But still, I don't know what to say."

She tugged on his shirt collar and winked. "It's easy. Just say *thank you.*"

He swallowed over a lump in his throat. "Thank you."

On the way back to Aileen, Healy reviewed his class schedule with Ellen, and they discussed how best to work out his transportation. As they had hoped, he could ride to campus with her for most of his classes, but a couple of his labs would require returning in the evening.

"You could apply for a driver's license, you know," Ellen suggested.

Healy smirked. "And drive what?"

Ellen looked at him with feigned astonishment. "Don't tell me you've already forgotten the proficiency of our esteemed prayer-chain coordinator. After all she's managed so far, I'm sure coming up with a vehicle would be small potatoes for her."

Warmth spread through Healy's chest as he pictured the fair-haired woman he fell more in love with every day. "She is something, that's for sure."

Ellen parked in the driveway, and they stepped through the side gate. "Thanks again for all your help," Healy said. "And remember, you promised to let me be the one to tell Valerie about Tom when the time is right."

Ellen made a zipping motion across her lips. "It'll be hard, but I'll try." She waved as Healy started up the stairs to his apartment.

Turning his key in the deadbolt, Healy realized with confusion that the door was already unlocked. He distinctly remembered locking the apartment before leaving with Ellen. Cautiously he pushed open the door and stepped inside. At the sight of the bright yellow banner taped across the archway, he broke into a grin.

"Oh, Val, you are really something."

He ducked under the banner and dropped his stack of college papers on the end table. On the other side of the coffee table, three inflated red balloons rolled aimlessly across the floor, propelled by the gentle breeze from the air conditioner. A cellophane bag containing more balloons lay on the sofa, along with a roll of masking tape and two unopened packages of crepe paper streamers.

An uneasy feeling tugged at Healy's insides. Had Valerie had another panic attack? She'd come so far, and the last thing she needed was a setback. He spun on his heel and hurried downstairs, thumping loudly on the Paiges' back door.

"Healy, come in." Ellen's worried look confirmed his fears. "Something's happened with Valerie. I found her shut in her room with Annie and Jean Franklin from next door, and she hasn't told any of us what's wrong. Maybe she'll talk to you."

Healy strode across the kitchen. "Did Annie say anything?"

"Just that they were decorating your apartment, and then Aunt Val started crying and said they had to leave. At least Val had the presence of mind to ask Jean to come over." Ellen hugged herself and stared toward the hallway. "I don't like this, Healy. She was doing so much better."

"Let me see what I can find out." He took a steadying breath before marching upstairs.

He paused outside Valerie's sitting room door. "Valerie? It's Healy. Can I come in?"

"Go away," came the muffled reply. "Please. Just go away."

"Valerie, I—"

The door opened slowly, and Jean slipped out with Annie clutching her hand. The latch clicked shut behind them. Annie looked up at Healy with a solemn frown. "You can't 'sturb Aunt Val right now. She's very sad."

Healy cast the silver-haired woman a searching look, and she shrugged. "All I know is, something upset Valerie enough that she didn't trust herself to take care of Annie. She phoned and asked if I could come over—first time she's ever needed to call on me, so I knew it must be serious. I asked her several times to let me phone Connor, but she didn't want me bothering him at the office."

Healy pulled a hand across his face. He knelt and caught Annie's small pink hands in his, squeezing them gently. "Sweetheart, do you know why Aunt Val is sad? Can you tell me what happened in my apartment?"

Her bottom lip trembled. "I think she got mad at me 'cause I was looking at your Bible. I'm real sorry, Healy. I didn't tear it, I promise. I just wanted to see if it had pictures like Daddy's."

Healy lowered his head. "Did Aunt Val look at my Bible, too?"

"Uh-huh." Annie's voice quavered, and he glanced up into worried blue eyes. "Are you mad at Aunt Val for looking at your Bible? Because she was real careful, and she put it right back on the table where it was."

He drew the child into his arms and stroked her pale yellow curls. "No, darlin', I'm not mad at you, and I'm not mad at Aunt Val."

Tiny arms wound around his neck. "Then can you make her happy again? We were gonna have a party for you 'cause you went to college with my mommy." She drew back and searched his face. "Did you see the big yellow sign? Did you like it?"

"I loved it." He swooped her up as he rose. "Tell you what. Let's go back downstairs and talk to Mommy."

"Shall I stay with Valerie?" Jean asked.

"I'd really appreciate it if you'd keep an eye on her for a while. Until we sort through this mess, I don't think she should be alone."

"I understand." Jean quietly re-entered the sitting room as Healy started downstairs.

He found Ellen pacing the kitchen, paring knife in one hand, a glossy green bell pepper in the other. She looked up anxiously. "Well?"

Healy set Annie on a kitchen chair and gave Ellen a meaningful look. "I think she knows."

"About you and Tom? But how?"

With a sidelong glance at Annie, he moved a few steps away and lowered his voice to tell Ellen about the inscription in his Bible and what Annie had said.

"But why would she be so upset?" Ellen plopped the pepper onto a cutting board. She stabbed the knife into it and sawed viciously around the stem. "This makes no sense, none at all. I mean, sure, she might be surprised, maybe even miffed at you for not telling her sooner. But even I remember Tom talking about an old friend he kept in touch with who was serving time. I should think Valerie would be happy to finally know who you are."

Healy slicked back his shaggy hair. "Maybe it's *because* I'm Tom's friend. Maybe it brings me too close." *Why, Lord? I wanted to be the one to tell her. Now what do I do?*

"Did you know my uncle Tom?" Annie asked. "I didn't. I wasn't even born yet when he went to live in heaven."

"Annie, why don't you go see what's on TV?" Ellen sent a forced smile her daughter's way. "Or pop in one of your Veggie Tales videos."

The little girl skipped out of the kitchen, and Healy sank onto the chair she had vacated. Ellen tossed her paring knife onto the cutting board at the same moment the doorbell rang. "It's probably the pastor," she said, starting toward the front door. "Maybe he can help."

Moments later Healy heard the jolly man's voice echoing in the hallway. "Ellen, my dear, hope I'm not too early. Is our college man all enrolled?"

Ellen's response was subdued. "Pastor, I'm afraid Valerie's had a setback."

Healy rose as Ellen escorted Pastor Henke into the kitchen. The white-haired man took Healy's hand and shook it. "Well, well. I thought I was coming for a celebratory dinner in your honor. But I gather we have something much more serious to contend with."

They all sat around the table, and Healy and Ellen took turns explaining to Pastor Henke what sketchy details they had pieced together.

When they finished, the pastor rubbed his chin and sighed. "Clearly Connor was wise to be so cautious about revealing Healy's friendship with Tom. But that knowledge alone shouldn't have produced a reaction this severe. No, there must be something more to it."

"But what?" Ellen spread her hands in a helpless gesture.

"I suspect," the pastor began thoughtfully, "that seeing Tom's inscription in Healy's Bible triggered a memory her subconscious mind has intentionally suppressed all this time."

"You may be right." Ellen moistened her lips and turned to Healy. "Valerie was seriously injured herself the night Tom died. Days went by before she could talk coherently to the police. By then, she couldn't remember—or else she didn't want to remember—exactly what happened. All we've ever known is based on the evidence the police found at the scene."

Healy rose, then stalked across the kitchen, hands jammed into his back pockets. "She *has* to talk to somebody. She can't go on like this."

"Don't you think we know that?" Ellen slapped the table. "From the day she got out of the hospital and came to live with us, we have all tried to convince her to continue therapy."

"I'm sorry." Healy tucked in his chin. "I know you have."

"Has anyone called Connor?" Pastor Henke asked.

Healy shook his head. "Jean said Valerie wouldn't let her."

"Then we must do so right away." When Ellen started to rise, the pastor placed a hand on her arm. "You're exhausted, my dear. Let me."

As Pastor Henke phoned Connor's office, Ellen cast an apologetic glance at Healy. "I didn't mean to snap at you. I know how much Valerie means to you."

"It's all right. I understand." He noticed the glass of fruit juice she had left on the counter and carried it to her. She smiled her thanks.

"Connor is finishing up with a patient and will be right home," Pastor Henke reported. "In the meantime, perhaps I should see if Valerie will speak to me."

"Yes, she trusts you." Ellen looked at him hopefully. "Please try."

The pastor disappeared up the stairs, and moments later

Jean Franklin peeked into the kitchen. "I wish I could have done more. I feel so helpless."

Ellen gave her neighbor a quick hug. "I'm just grateful you were there when she called."

"Me, too. Please let me know how she's doing."

"I will." She thanked Jean again, and the woman slipped out.

Healy returned to his chair and pressed his palms into his eye sockets. "This is my fault. If I'd told Valerie everything from the start, this would never have happened."

"You can't know that for sure," Ellen said. "If discovering your identity did trigger Valerie's memory of the night Tom was killed, *when* she found out wouldn't have made a difference. The memories themselves are the problem here, not you."

Again Healy leaped to his feet. The chair scraped backward across the floor. "How do you know?" he shouted. "How do you know I'm not the whole problem? Tom died a violent death at the hands of criminals. I'm a criminal. I killed somebody, too."

Breathing hard, he stormed out the door. Beating a man to death was the biggest mistake of his life. Coming to Aileen was the second. He knew what he had to do.

thirteen

Darkness settled over the Paige house. Silent tears streaming down her cheeks, Valerie capped her fountain pen and laid it on the blank page. Words had failed her tonight; not even the comforting ritual of pouring her heart into her journal could soothe her troubled spirit. Wearily she rose and leaned her head against the bookcase Healy had built.

Oh, Healy. . .Healy, why you?

"Healy is not to blame," a gentle voice reminded her.

"I know, Lord, but still. . ."

No one could understand. Not Pastor Henke with his godly wisdom and prayers, nor Connor and his relentless attempts to break down her resistance to counseling. Especially not Ellen, whose life as wife, mother, and teacher continued full and happy.

"We all have our own prisons." Healy's words.

"I did not choose this prison." Her fists knotted. "Lord, I don't want to live any longer in fear and isolation. I don't want to live without love."

"Then forgive."

For the life of her, she thought she had—years ago. When the trial began several months after Tom's death, the judge excused her from court appearances because of her persistent back pain and the debilitating anxiety attacks. Instead, both the defense and prosecuting attorneys deposed her on videotape. She said what she had to say and then tried to put the trial out of her mind. It seemed the only way she could function without losing her mind completely.

Many weeks later, the assistant district attorney paid her another visit. She listened stoically as he informed her the three men had been convicted and sentenced to lengthy prison terms, including a life sentence for her assailant, the man who was also driving the getaway car. Valerie had expected some sense of finality, but she'd felt only emptiness.

As the attorney got up to leave, Valerie remembered something she had read in an inspirational book her mother had sent her. She reached for the man's arm. "Do you. . .have photographs of the men?"

He looked askance at her. "Why?"

"I need to see their faces. It will help me try to forgive them."

Searching his briefcase, he pulled out photocopies of the men's police mug shots. "If you say so," he said, handing them to her. "But if you can forgive these guys after all they took from you, you're a better person than I'll ever be."

"If I don't forgive them, in the Lord's eyes I'm no better than they are."

Every day for months afterward, she purposefully studied the photos, memorizing their faces and praying over each one. "Jesus, grant me the strength to forgive. Take away my anger and fear, and help me to desire Your love and goodness for each of these men. Lead them to repentance. Show them the blessed life they could have in knowing You."

She'd struggled at first, her voice tear-choked and her heart full of bitterness and doubt. She remembered the day she finally knew in her soul the forgiveness for which she prayed. It was mid-October, almost a year to the day after Tom's death. Still suffering from recurring back pain, she had been propped up in bed, reading her Bible. A verse from Isaiah 49 leaped out at her:

"Can a mother forget the baby at her breast and have no compassion on the child she has borne? Though she may forget, I will not forget you! See, I have engraved you on the palms of my hands; your walls are ever before me. Your sons hasten back, and those who laid you waste depart from you."

God's reassurance of His everlasting justice and mercy rang out through the words. He had not forgotten her in her sorrow and never would. God alone would deal with those who had hurt her. And in precious memories He would restore to her what she had lost.

Laying the Bible aside, she had eased out of bed and limped to the closet. She tugged some things aside until she found the flat box containing the cream-colored leather-bound journal Tom had given her less than a month before he died.

"This is a special time, my sweet Lady V," he'd told her with a kiss. "I thought you might want to keep a diary of your thoughts and feelings. Someday," he said, gently patting her rounded belly, "those words may mean a lot to the little one growing in there."

Continually busy at the restaurant, she had never gotten around to writing in the journal, and after the night she lost everything important to her, she had seen no reason to. But on the day she had finally sensed God's love and forgiveness settling around her heart, she knew the time for remembering had come. From then on, writing in the journal became a sacrament of remembrance. In the sanctuary of those lined white pages, she found expression for both the agony of her double loss and the joy of eternal hope.

Now she must learn to forgive all over again. "O Father," she said, moving from the bookcase to the window, "I love Healy with all my heart. I don't want his connection with Tom's death to come between us. Help me."

The apartment windows were dark. Perhaps Healy was still downstairs with Ellen and Connor. They must all be so worried. She had to talk to them, to apologize to Healy, to explain.

Muted voices led her to the den. Pausing at the door, she glimpsed Ellen curled on the sofa, resting in Connor's arms.

"If she won't talk to anyone, what else can we do?" Ellen flicked away a tear.

"Just pray, I guess. Maybe in the morning—" Connor glanced up. "Val."

She entered shyly. "I'm sorry I worried everyone."

Connor rose and enveloped her in his arms. "Sis, whatever happened, you need to talk to us. You can't keep holding it inside."

"I know." She drew comfort from the softness of his cotton shirt. "I just needed time to sort through it all."

Ellen laid a hand on her shoulder. "Val honey, did you remember something?"

Valerie pressed a hand to her mouth, a sob choking her. "I need to talk to Healy. Do you know where he is?"

Connor and Ellen exchanged glances. "He's. . .he's gone," Connor said.

"Gone?" Valerie shook her head. "What are you saying?"

"Connor tried to stop him—we both did—but he packed his things and left with Pastor Henke a couple of hours ago." Ellen's eyes brimmed. "He kept saying it was his fault, and he didn't want to hurt you anymore."

"But it *isn't* his fault." Valerie sank into a chair, despair overwhelming her.

Connor sat on the edge of the sofa and reached for her hand. "Valerie, it's time you told us exactly what's going on here. Is it. . .do you know about Healy and Tom?"

She nodded, unable to speak.

Connor cast Ellen a knowing glance. "Healy realized you must have figured it out when you looked in his Bible."

"What happened?" Ellen pleaded. "Did it trigger your memories from the night of the accident?"

Again she nodded. Tears coursed down her cheeks.

"Oh, honey." Ellen knelt in front of her. "What did you remember that could be worse than what we already know?"

She took a steadying breath. "Tom crossed the street that night to mail a letter to Gus—to Healy. If he hadn't, we'd have gone straight to our car. Tom would still be alive."

She pressed a hand to her abdomen, her voice choked with emotion. "And so would our baby."

❧

Healy awoke from a fitful sleep, forgetting for a moment that he was no longer at the apartment. He set his bare feet on the plush carpeting of Pastor Henke's guest bedroom and exhaled tiredly. Life without Valerie seemed unthinkable, but he would not cause her more pain, and if that meant leaving Aileen, so be it.

Now, if only he could figure out what God wanted him to do next. Unfortunately, the Lord had been strangely silent since last night.

Maybe a hot shower would help. He took his shaving kit and a change of clothes from his duffel bag and trudged to the bathroom. When he emerged twenty minutes later, the aroma of brewing coffee lured him to the kitchen.

"Good morning, my boy." Pastor Henke cracked an egg into a bowl. "Oh my, you had a bad night, didn't you?"

Healy helped himself to a cup of coffee and took a seat in the sunny breakfast nook. "I feel like my whole life has been ripped out from under me. . .again."

"I'm sure you do." The white-haired pastor fumbled through a drawer and pulled out a wire whisk as butter sizzled in a skillet. After beating the eggs, he poured them into the skillet. "These won't take long. Would you start some toast, please?"

Healy dropped two slices of wheat bread into the toaster. "I promise I won't trouble you for long. As soon as I find another place, I'll be on my way."

"And where exactly do you plan on going?"

"People from your church have invested in my education, and I don't intend to let them down. But I can't stay in Aileen, not if it means upsetting Valerie. I thought I'd look for a place over near the college. Maybe find some work there, too."

Pastor Henke waved a spatula. "Healy Ferguson, I gave you

more credit. Have you no faith that God can work out whatever difficulties lie between you and Valerie?"

Healy sighed and stared out the window. "It isn't that I don't trust God, Pastor. I just don't trust my own judgment anymore. At least not where Valerie's concerned."

"Humph. All the more reason you should not be jumping to conclusions and going off half-cocked." Pastor Henke divided the scrambled eggs onto two plates and carried them to the table. When the toast popped, Healy handed a slice to the pastor and methodically spread butter and jam across the second one for himself. They ate in thoughtful silence.

Finally Pastor Henke spoke. "Healy, do you recall what you told me the day we first met?"

Healy sipped his coffee. "I said a lot of things."

"Yes, but what stands out in my mind is how certain you were of God's hand being with you every mile of your journey, from getting on the bus to St. Louis, to seeing the advertisement for Zion Community Church, to finding your way to my office here in Aileen."

"It all seemed right. . .then." Healy pushed his empty plate away. "But that was before I knew Valerie was Tom's wife. Before I started falling in love with her. Before something—God knows what—made her shut me out."

The phone rang. Pastor Henke angled a concerned glance toward Healy as he spoke to the caller. "Yes, he's right here. Hold on." He handed the receiver to Healy. "It's Connor."

Healy's throat tightened as he took the phone. "Hello?"

"Hi, Healy. How are you?" The tension edging Connor's voice belied his polite greeting.

"Okay." As far as Healy was concerned, Connor could cut the small talk and say what he had to say. It couldn't be good. "How are things there?" he asked, meaning Valerie.

"Better, I think. Valerie finally talked to us last night." Connor released a pent-up breath. "Healy, she wants you to know why she reacted the way she did."

"Like I don't already know? I'm a loser, and she finally figured it out."

"No, it's not that at all. Here, let me put her on—"

"Don't. I can't talk to her."

"All right, then, you'll have to hear it from me."

Healy forced himself to listen. His remorse only intensified as Connor related Valerie's recaptured memories of the night Tom died. And he recalled—suddenly in vivid detail—the last letter he'd ever received from his faithful friend. Tom had rambled on and on about soon becoming a father. *"Never thought it would happen to me,"* he wrote. *"Can't wait to see what kind of amazing creation God's going to bring from a crusty, black-haired part-Italian and a sweet little blond Irish girl."*

Healy covered his eyes. "Oh, dear Lord, forgive me." Would he never stop paying for a sixteen-year-old mistake? How could he live with himself knowing Valerie had lost her husband, lost her baby, all on account of Tom's devotion to a man who in no way deserved it?

Connor spoke firmly. "Valerie doesn't blame you, Healy. None of us do. She feels terrible about yesterday. She wants you to come back."

Muffled voices sounded in the background. "Here, Valerie wants to tell you herself. I'm giving her the phone."

"No—"

"Healy."

He dissolved at the sound of her voice.

"Healy, please—I'm sorry. I never wanted to hurt you." She released a small sob. "This is too hard over the phone. Come back so I can explain."

Healy took a shuddering breath, almost choking on his next words. "I'm not good for you. You deserve better. Please. Don't call me again."

"Healy, wait—"

"Good-bye, Valerie." He hung up the telephone before he could change his mind.

≥

Stunned, Valerie handed Connor's desk phone back to him. Tears filled her eyes. "He hung up on me."

Connor circled the desk and hugged her. "Give him some time. Finding out the truth has been a shock for both of you."

Valerie eased out of her brother's embrace and turned to the window. Along the eaves of the front porch, thirsty petunias drooped from their hanging baskets. The grass near the curb looked brown and dry. It was not yet nine o'clock, and already waves of heat shimmered off the pavement. The whole landscape looked as parched and desolate as the wilderness of her heart.

"It's been almost five years, Connor. I've wasted so much time hiding from the truth. I couldn't face knowing Tom's faithfulness to someone I'd never even met cost me everything I held dear."

"Tom's friendship with Healy isn't what killed him or your baby. Three criminals fleeing from the law killed them."

"I know. Deep inside, I know." She moved her head slowly from side to side, her hands curling into tight fists. "Oh, Connor, I wish you'd never told him about the letter. The pain in his voice—I can't even bear to think about how much he's suffering now."

"He's with the pastor. He couldn't be in better hands." Connor gently smoothed Valerie's knotted fists. "God's going to see both of you through this, I'm certain."

"I know, but. . ." How did that old cliché go—one step forward, two steps back? That's how her life felt lately. It was an old game, and she was tired of it. Things had to change.

Lord, help me. Help me take the next step forward.

She tilted her head to look up into her brother's shimmering blue eyes. With effort, she sent him a weak smile. "I honestly wasn't ready before," she said, finally understanding why, "but now I think I am. It's time I got serious about some counseling."

fourteen

Under the glow of the brass chandelier, Healy sat at the pastor's kitchen table and studied his math book. High-school algebra stumped him as a teenager. He found it no easier in his thirties to comprehend how x's and y's could stand for actual numbers, much less how he was supposed to figure out what those numbers were.

Pastor Henke laid a hand on his shoulder. "Looks as if you're experiencing a slight case of dyscalculia."

Healy rolled his eyes. Where did the pastor come up with these words? "If that means I can't do algebra, you're right. Maybe I should just stick to carpentry." He tossed his pencil onto a sheet of notebook paper worn thin by frequent erasures.

"Of course you are never required to use algebra when constructing something with hammer and nails, correct?" The pastor settled into a chair and looked expectantly at Healy.

Healy stared back at the pastor. "Well, Jesus was a carpenter, and I don't recall one single reference in the Bible about Him studying algebra."

Pastor Henke drew his eyebrows together. "You don't think math was involved in multiplying five loaves and two fishes to feed the five thousand? Or what about our Lord's instruction about how many times you should forgive your brother when he sins against you?"

"Seventy times seven. Okay, I get the message." Healy sat back and rubbed his eyes. "But I still don't get this x-equals-y stuff."

"You've been back in school less than a month, after how many years? Don't be so hard on yourself. It'll come."

Maybe, Healy thought as the pastor left him to his studies, but even if he did manage to earn any kind of college degree, would it matter? At this point, he felt as if he were merely going through the motions, and only because he refused to disappoint those who had so caringly expressed confidence in him—not the least of whom was Pastor Henke.

Healy had insisted several times that he should find his own place, but the pastor would not even acknowledge such discussions. "My dear wife has been with the Lord nearly ten years now," the man had reasoned, "and our children live out of state. It gets rather lonely around here, and besides, you need some time to get your feet on the ground and develop a sound financial strategy for your future."

Strategy? The only "financial strategy" he ever had was to make sure he always had at least two bills to rub together in his wallet. And sometimes even that was hard to manage.

In the end, he had finally agreed to live rent-free in the pastor's guestroom in exchange for doing various odd jobs around the house. Ellen also insisted on driving him to school as planned until he got a license and afford his own car. Pastor Henke or another church member provided transportation to his evening classes. Though his new friends from Zion patiently explained time and again that they expected nothing in return, he made them promise to call on him for any home maintenance chores he could help with.

Still, all enthusiasm had vanished the day he walked out of Valerie's life. Not even Pastor Henke's steadfast support and Ellen's continued friendship could fill the void.

As he stared unseeing at the math book, he realized if he made it through college—if he made anything at all of this second chance he'd been given—he would have to do it for himself and for God.

With a determined sigh, he picked up his pencil and tackled the algebra problem once more. Amazingly, it suddenly made sense. His brain cranked out the solution in a matter of minutes, and he mouthed a silent "*Hallelujah!*"

"Well, well." Pastor Henke, returning to the kitchen, paused to adjust his tie. "Is that a smile of victory I see?"

"I may survive this class after all." Healy yawned and stretched. "You're all dressed up. Headed out this late?"

The pastor's expression turned grim. "Yes, I'm afraid so. Young Tina Maxwell goes to court in a few days, and I'm going to visit her at the detention center and try to offer some encouragement."

Healy recalled his conversations with the pastor about a teenager who'd been picked up for shoplifting with the daughter of one of Zion's families. "I'm sure she's very scared," he said. How could he forget his own terror upon entering the courtroom to face judge and jury, knowing they held the rest of his life in their hands?

"Indeed she is." Pastor Henke picked up his car keys and Bible from the kitchen counter. "But just when I think I'm breaking through her shell, she closes herself off again."

Healy shut his math book and placed his assignment in the pocket of a green folder. "At least she hasn't told you to stop visiting. That's a positive sign."

"It should be, I know, but I'm so far removed from her, both in age and experience." The pastor narrowed his eyes at Healy. "But you, on the other hand. . . Healy my boy, can I persuade you to accompany me tonight?"

"Aw, Pastor, I don't know." Healy extended one leg and stared at his dirt-stained sneaker. "You're trained in this kind of thing. I'm not. Besides, what would I say to a teenage girl?"

"You only need some common ground and a compassionate heart." The pastor pulled out a chair and sat down, resting an elbow on the table. He leaned close and looked Healy in the eye. "And have you already forgotten your extraordinary success helping Valerie conquer her anxieties? I've watched you with little Annie, too. The child adores you."

The mention of Valerie and Annie tore at the empty place in his soul. "I don't have any special knack. It was only because

I know what fear feels like. I cared, and I wanted to help."

"That's exactly what I'm talking about." Fixing Healy with a thoughtful gaze, the pastor rubbed his chin. "I don't know why this never occurred to me before. You have incredible people skills, Healy. Others instinctively trust you—your openness, your honesty, your genuine concern. This is a God-given gift, and you would be remiss not to use it in His service."

Healy rubbed perspiring hands on his jeans. Part of him wanted to deny everything the pastor had said, but when he examined his heart, he realized helping others had been his constant goal ever since he came to know Christ in prison.

As if reading his thoughts, Pastor Henke said, "Remember when you first came to Aileen and I phoned the penitentiary to confirm your story? The chaplain's letter told about all the inmates you had brought to Christ, all the lives you helped to turn around."

He laid a hand on Healy's arm. "And my conversation with the warden was no different. He held you up as a model prisoner, going the second mile with every task, taking advantage of vocational training, helping new inmates avoid trouble, even risking injury yourself to break up the inevitable fights."

Instinctively Healy's right hand covered the long, ugly scar streaking across his left forearm. As if it were yesterday, he remembered forcing himself between a huge, angry convict and a cowering new arrival who'd made the mistake of crossing the big man's path. Without warning, the big man whipped out a shiv—a piece of jagged glass taped to the handle of a spoon stolen from the cafeteria. Before Healy could dodge the makeshift weapon, he felt it slash through his arm and watched his own blood pour out on the asphalt of the exercise yard. The wound had required twenty-nine stitches to close. He'd felt and counted every one.

"So what do you say, Healy?" the pastor asked. "Will you go with me to talk to Tina?"

Maybe helping someone else was exactly what he needed.

Maybe in some small way it could make him feel useful again. "All right, Pastor, if you really think I can help."

❧

After joining Connor and Ellen to hear Annie's bedtime prayers, Valerie slipped out to the back porch and settled into a wicker rocker. Crickets and cicadas serenaded the muggy twilight; heat lightning flickered on the horizon. She wished the signs portended rain, but the weatherman on the six o'clock news had offered no hope for a break from the intense drought under which the entire Midwest baked.

At least she could be outdoors in the dark again and not feel afraid. The counselor Connor had found, a soft-spoken Christian woman, truly seemed to be helping. For the first several visits, Dr. Miller came to the house, but as Valerie gradually recovered the ground Healy had helped her gain over the summer, the doctor encouraged her to attempt the trip to her office. Today Connor had driven Valerie to her first appointment there, and in spite of a shaky start and arriving forty-five minutes late, she had somehow managed to hold herself together.

Thank You, Lord, thank You, she prayed in rhythm with the creak of the chair.

She glanced up at the sound of the back door and smiled to see her sister-in-law.

Ellen drew a chair closer. "Is this a private party, or can anyone join in?"

"You're welcome to stay if you can stand the heat."

"If I were any more pregnant, I probably couldn't." Ellen settled into the cushioned chair with a contented sigh. "Connor said you did great today. We're very proud of you."

"Dr. Miller is wonderful. She seems to sense exactly how much I can handle."

Ellen reached across the space between them and gave Valerie's hand a squeeze. "Connor and I have been praying for this ever since you came to live with us."

They rocked in silence for several minutes, until Valerie could no longer hold back the question she had wanted to ask for weeks. "Ellen, how is Healy?"

Ellen cleared her throat. "His classes seem to be going okay, except for math. He has his nose buried in his book on the way to and from campus almost every day." Crossing her legs, she continued, "Now his carpentry class is another story. Word around campus is that he can out-carpenter the instructor. I wouldn't be surprised—"

"I mean, how *is* he?" Valerie fixed Ellen with a look. "Please, how's he doing. . .in here?" She pressed a hand to her heart.

"I don't know how to answer that question." Ellen angled her a sideways glance. "He obviously misses you terribly, though he won't talk about it, at least to me."

Valerie rose and leaned on the porch rail, staring across the shadowy backyard. A mockingbird's strident call sounded from near the top of one of the oak trees.

She spun around. "I don't understand why he won't at least talk to me."

Ellen leaned over the arm of her chair to pinch a brown leaf off a wilting ivy plant. "What does Dr. Miller say?"

"She says we both need some space to heal." Valerie's tone became flippant. "That's such a cliché. 'I need my space.' Well, I tried hiding inside my own little 'space' and still never healed completely. Opening my heart to Healy became my first real glimmer of hope."

She lifted her hands. "And now everyone's telling me *Healy* needs space. Why did he have to pull away from me just when I find myself coming fully alive again?"

Ellen didn't answer, and Valerie knew how selfish and unfair she sounded. But when she glanced toward the dark windows of the garage apartment, she missed Healy more than ever. She sank onto a step and buried her face in her hands.

Dear heavenly Father, please watch over Healy. You know his needs. You know the desires of his heart. I only want what's best

*for him, so I ask You to help me accept whatever decisions he makes
about his life. . .even if those decisions don't include me.*

🙣

Several days later Healy rose from his seat near the back of
Zion Community Church as Pastor Henke announced the
closing hymn. He'd attended a few times with Connor and
Ellen over the summer, but not consistently. More often he
had preferred to join Valerie in her sitting room on Sunday
mornings to read and discuss Bible passages with her. He
found her love for the Lord inspiring, and he could listen for
hours as she read from scripture in her quietly firm, expressive
voice.

Since moving in with the pastor, he'd become a regular at
Zion. Although he remained shy about meeting people, he
encountered many warm and friendly individuals. He couldn't
help silently speculating about which members had anony-
mously made it possible for him to enroll in college.

After Pastor Henke pronounced the benediction, Healy
placed his hymnal in the rack and turned to step into the aisle.
A small, dark-haired man in a tan polo shirt blocked his way.

"Mr. Ferguson?"

Healy nodded. The man looked familiar, but for a moment
Healy couldn't place him. "If I should know you, I'm sorry. I've
met so many new people lately."

"Ed Maxwell, Tina's father." He extended his hand. "I want
to thank you for all you've done for her."

"Of course. We met at Tina's hearing." Warmth spread
through Healy's chest as he took Mr. Maxwell's hand. "How's
she doing, sir? I heard about her sentencing." The girl had
received one month in juvenile detention and one year's pro-
bation with community service.

"It could have been a lot worse if not for you." Mr. Maxwell
crushed Healy's knuckles in his tenacious grip. "Your coming
to court and putting in a good word for her—I know that's
what made the difference with the judge."

Healy waved away the man's praise. "I'm sure the judge saw what we already knew. Tina hasn't been in serious trouble before. She's young, and she made a stupid mistake. She learned her lesson and has every intention of staying out of trouble from now on."

"Yes, but it took both you and Pastor Henke to get through to her in the first place." The man blinked brimming eyes. "I still can't get over the fact that perfect strangers would take an interest in my daughter. I mean, Pastor Henke came to see Tina while she was still in the hospital after the car accident. And then you both visited her regularly at the detention center."

"The pastor's a good man. I'd hate to think where I'd be today if not for him."

"Well, he's the reason I'm in church today." Mr. Maxwell glanced toward Pastor Henke as the elderly man worked his way down the aisle, greeting people along the way. "Actually, both of you are. After Tina's mother divorced me, I pretty much gave up on God. That's when Tina first started acting out—just little signs of rebellion then, but if I'd had any idea what it would lead to. . . Anyway, you and the pastor have reminded me what Christ's love is all about."

Mr. Maxwell lowered his voice. "Truth is, I almost turned around and walked out this morning when I saw the Sandersons sitting there with Marsha like nothing had happened, while my Tina's locked up. But then I thought, God loves them, too. And we're all sinners, right? That's what church is for."

"You're right. People like the Sandersons may have a different way of handling their problems, but at least they're here, and God will keep working on their hearts."

"Yeah, I hope so. Well, I just wanted to say thanks. Nice talking to you." Mr. Maxwell gave Healy's now bloodless hand a final squeeze before departing.

As Healy jiggled his fingers to restore feeling, Connor and Ellen walked over, Annie between them. He couldn't help noticing the slight bulge of Ellen's pregnancy beneath her loose-fitting black-and-beige print dress.

"Don't worry, I won't shake your hand," Connor said with a chuckle. "Who was that man, anyway?"

When Healy explained it was Tina Maxwell's father, both Connor and Ellen gave him a knowing look.

"Pastor Henke told us how great you were with Tina," Ellen remarked.

"It felt good to be able to help."

A tiny hand tugged on his pants leg. "Healy, when are you coming back to my house? I miss you."

He caught Ellen's apologetic glance as he knelt to give Annie a hug. "I see you in church every Sunday now, sweetie." He gave her corkscrew curls a gentle tug. "Afraid that's the best I can do for now."

"Is it 'cause you're going to college? My mommy goes to the college, and she lives at my house. Why can't you live there anymore?"

"I'm sorry," Connor said. "We've tried to explain, but what can I say? My daughter is smitten with you."

"And she's not the only one," Ellen muttered.

Connor jabbed her with his elbow, and she shot him an exasperated glare.

Healy pretended not to notice as he stood upright again. Relief swept over him when he saw Pastor Henke approaching.

"I saw Mr. Maxwell talking to you." The pastor loosened the knotted rope at the waist of his white cassock. "So good to see the man in church today."

"Did you get a chance to speak with him?"

"Yes, for a few moments, but he was in a hurry to visit Tina." He turned to Connor. "Any Sunday now, I expect to see our dear Valerie accompany you to church."

"Us, too. At the rate things are progressing, I think she'll be ready very soon."

Pastor Henke beamed. "I'm so glad. I hear the counseling

sessions are going extremely well."

Ellen put her arm around Connor's waist and looked straight at Healy. "Better than we ever dared hope. She's so looking forward to living a full life again."

A suffocating heaviness pressed down upon Healy. He edged toward the door. "Sorry, would you excuse me, please? I, uh, I really need some air."

At the far end of the rapidly emptying parking lot, he leaned against Pastor Henke's red Mustang. The noonday sun raised beads of perspiration on his forehead as he looked toward the gold cross atop Zion's white steeple.

Dear Jesus, please help them understand. Especially Valerie. And please help me get it right this time.

For several days now, he'd been preoccupied with a scripture he'd come across in the book of James: "Perseverance must finish its work so that you may be mature and complete, not lacking anything." Until he became a whole person himself, he could not give himself fully to Valerie or any other woman.

He had only recently come to understand how incomplete he remained. Even knowing he had full forgiveness in Christ, he struggled for years with the need to atone for taking the life of another human being. He once thought he'd feel whole again after serving out his prison sentence. Last year, when the prison gates closed behind him for the last time, he decided his life would not be complete until he could finally leave Michigan, find Tom, and thank him for literally saving his life. When he amazingly discovered himself falling in love with Valerie and realized she loved him, too, he hoped he'd at last find wholeness in this extraordinary new relationship.

Finally, God showed him that completeness had to begin on the inside. His security, his salvation, his very worth as a human being must have only one source: the Lord.

fifteen

Valerie pressed perspiring hands against her thighs. Her wide-eyed gaze darted side to side through the windows of Ellen's Mazda. "There are so many people. We shouldn't have picked a Saturday. I don't think I can do this."

"Then you'll have to sit out here and fry, because this is the only day I had off this week and I'm not leaving the engine running for you." Yanking her keys from the ignition, Ellen shoved open the car door and stepped out into the Wal-Mart parking lot.

A blast of heat rushed in, and Valerie sucked in her breath. "Ellen Paige, you are the meanest woman alive."

Peering through the open door, Ellen shot Valerie a challenging look. "Dr. Miller said you were ready for this. Are you going to flunk your homework assignment? Because I'm not signing your excuse this time."

Valerie made a growling sound in her throat. "Okay, okay. I'll. . .try."

As the next step in getting Valerie out of the house, Dr. Miller had given her a choice: a brief shopping trip, or accompany her family to church. Stupidly, she imagined shopping would be easier, without the added embarrassment of facing people she knew in case she suddenly found herself in the grip of a panic attack.

She flung open her door, instantly regretting her carelessness when it scraped against a shiny black Ford Explorer in the adjacent space. A warning *beep* sounded from the hulking vehicle. Valerie clambered out and examined the Explorer for damage.

Ellen stalked around to Valerie's side of the car. "Do I need to get out my insurance card?"

Valerie rubbed her hand along the car door. "I think it's okay. Don't see any—"

"You are standing too close to the vehicle. Move away at once."

At the computerized warning, Valerie sprang back in astonishment. "Did you hear that?"

Ellen grabbed her arm. "Let's just do our shopping, okay?"

"But that car talked to me." Valerie glared over her shoulder as her sister-in-law tugged her toward the Wal-Mart entrance.

"It can talk all it wants as long as it doesn't mention any names when its owner comes back. Hurry up, it's hot out here."

A welcome gust of cool air greeted them inside. Before Valerie could react to the bright fluorescent lighting and the hordes of Saturday shoppers, Ellen thrust a shopping cart in front of her. "Here, push. It'll give you something to do." She rested a hand on Valerie's shoulder and added in a gentler tone, "And don't forget to breathe."

Breathe. Memories of Healy's encouraging smile and soothingly persuasive voice flooded her thoughts. She fought the lump in her throat and tried to concentrate on steering the cart.

"You're doing great," Ellen assured her. "Turn up this aisle."

Valerie clutched the cool blue cart handle. "What are we shopping for? I already forgot."

"Clothes for Annie, golf balls for Connor." Ellen paused and consulted her list. "And I need some blush, conditioner, and raspberry tea."

Valerie nodded, mentally repeating the list and trying to match the items with the store's information signs. *Keep your mind busy. You can do this.*

"What do you think of this?" Ellen held up a bright yellow children's shorts outfit with a watermelon appliqué. "It's on sale. Summer closeout, 50 percent off."

Valerie looked toward the ceiling. "I don't believe you. With Connor's and your combined income, why do you even care about bargain hunting?"

"Because it's *fun.*" Ellen grabbed another outfit off the rack. "This is adorable. Annie will love the little poodle on the front. And see, since they're on sale, I can buy twice as many for the same price."

Twenty minutes and four outfits for Annie later, Ellen scurried over to a display of ladies' swimsuits. She snatched up a slinky tropical-print tank suit. "Valerie, this is absolutely *you.*"

Intent on watching Ellen's shopping exploits, Valerie had relaxed considerably. She leaned on the shopping cart and narrowed her eyes. "And, oh, look," she said dryly, "it's marked down 75 percent. Seriously, where would I wear something like that?"

"Connor and I have been talking about putting in a pool." She fanned herself dramatically. "Especially after this summer. The fitting room is right here. Try it on, okay?"

Valerie couldn't remember the last time she'd shopped for herself except from a catalogue or online. Even more, she'd missed the girlish fun of a shopping expedition with another woman. She took another quick inventory of her emotional state. No shortness of breath, only the slightest flutter in her chest—but that could just be excitement. Yes, she was managing pretty well. And what could happen in a fitting room?

She bit her lip and took the bathing suit from Ellen. "Okay, I'll try it on, but I draw the line at coming out here to model for you."

Ellen grinned. "Fair enough. I'll wait for you right outside the door."

An attendant pointed Valerie to a vacant stall. She let out a long sigh as she closed the door, the tiny cubicle restoring her sense of security. Hanging the bathing suit on a hook, she took a moment to reorient herself before slipping out of her sundress.

As she donned the skimpy swimsuit, her excitement returned. Though she hadn't been able to be as physically active since the accident, the ten or fifteen minutes she attempted on Connor's treadmill several times a week had obviously kept her in pretty good shape. She looked at her figure from every possible angle and realized she liked what she saw. "I wonder if—"

She groaned. No matter how hard she tried, she could not get Healy Ferguson out of her mind. *Dear Lord, please, if it's Your will, bring him back to me. Soon.*

Wearing her sundress again, she sank onto the narrow bench and fumbled with a confusing array of slides and clips to reattach the swimsuit to the hanger. She became vaguely aware of a muted conversation going on in the cubicle next to hers.

"Just stick them in your purse. They're small enough," a young voice said.

"I don't know. . . . What if we get caught?"

"We won't. I've done this a hundred times. Do you want the bikini or not?"

"But the attendant counted how many items we brought in. She'll know if we don't bring them all back."

"It's Saturday. There's a million people here. She's too busy to notice anything." An exasperated sigh. "Come on. Just do it."

The fine hairs rose on the back of Valerie's neck. She gathered up her purse and the swimsuit and slipped into the passageway. Taking a steadying breath, she approached the attendant. "Excuse me, but you should probably call security. I think you have a problem in cubicle number 11."

The plump woman tossed a handful of empty hangers into a box below her counter and turned with a distracted sigh. "What kind of problem, ma'am?"

"I heard two girls—"

Ellen caught her arm. "Valerie, is everything all right?"

Laughter rang out in the passageway behind her. She turned to see two teenagers sauntering their way, each carrying several different articles of clothing.

The tall, auburn-haired girl plopped her stack on the counter. "None of these fit," she stated. "Come on, Jackie, let's go to the mall."

Acting on pure instinct, Valerie blocked their way. "My, you sure seem to be in a hurry." She couldn't miss the deer-in-the-headlights look in the eyes of the girl called Jackie. Glancing toward the attendant, she said, "I suggest you count the items they're returning and make sure they're all there."

"Lady, you should mind your own business," the first girl said, glaring at Valerie.

Ellen stepped closer now. "Well, hello, Marsha. Do your parents know you're out shopping today?"

"Marsha Sanderson?" Valerie suddenly recognized the girl from the church pictorial directory. She shook her head in dismay. "Oh, honey."

"Jackie, keep walking. They can't do anything." Marsha gripped her friend by the elbow. As the attendant picked up the phone, the girls dashed out of the dressing room.

"Come on, Val, you're a witness." Ellen parked her shopping cart next to the attendant's desk and told the woman she'd be back for it, then grabbed Valerie's hand.

Adrenalin pounded in Valerie's ears by the time they reached the exit. A burly uniformed man jogged over just as Marsha and Jackie plowed between the security gates, setting off a strident alarm. With Valerie and Ellen falling in behind him, the guard chased the girls outside. He caught up with them at Marsha's car, illegally parked in a handicapped spot.

Jackie started crying hysterically. "I didn't mean to go through with it, honestly." She dumped the contents of her large shoulder bag on the hood of the car and tossed a crumpled wad of green and yellow bikini parts at the security guard. "Please don't call my parents. They'll kill me. I'll never do it again, I swear."

"I don't have a choice, young lady." The security guard turned to Marsha and asked to see the contents of her handbag.

"I don't have to show you anything," she said smugly. "I know my rights."

"Fine. You can do it here, or you can do it down at the police station." He keyed the TALK button on his two-way radio and requested a patrol car be sent over. "It's pretty hot out here. Let's all take a walk inside to my nice, air-conditioned security office, shall we?"

After giving statements to the police and finally completing their shopping, Ellen and Valerie emerged from the Wal-Mart. They crossed the scorching parking lot and found Ellen's Mazda, now steamy from sitting under the sun.

"Dear Lord," Ellen muttered as she turned on the air conditioner full blast, "You can put an end to this heat any time now. Have You noticed it's October?"

Valerie felt as if she'd been run over by an army tank. She let her head drop against the headrest. "I think I should get triple credit for this assignment."

"I think Dr. Miller would agree." Ellen backed out of the parking space. "But just think, kiddo." She tapped Valerie's arm with the back of her hand. "You came out of this ordeal with a really cute swimsuit."

"Which I will never get to wear since I am planning to immediately go back into permanent hibernation."

"Come on, you did great." Ellen turned onto the highway heading toward Aileen. "I mean, how many recovering PTSD sufferers can say they faced down a talking car, cleaned out Wal-Mart's sale racks, and single-handedly captured two shoplifters all in the same day?"

Valerie puckered her lips. "I can't believe Marsha Sanderson almost got off scot-free again."

"The girl is clever, I'll give her that. At least now we know her modus operandi."

"Yeah, get your friend to steal the merchandise so you're never caught with it."

"But this time you can testify to what you overheard in the dressing room. With an actual witness, it won't be so easy for her daddy's expensive lawyers to get her off the hook."

A new fear clutched at Valerie's throat. She shot her sister-in-law a terrified look. "They'll summon me to court, won't they?"

"Let's deal with this one step at a time. God will help you do whatever you need to do when the time comes."

Valerie nodded, knowing her sister-in-law was right. She closed her eyes and made an effort to relax. When Ellen nudged her a short while later, she awoke in amazement to discover they were sitting in the driveway at home. She'd actually calmed herself enough to fall asleep in the car. *Praise God!*

≈

"Healy, the brakes, the brakes—*now!*"

"All right already." Healy stomped on the brake pedal of Pastor Henke's Mustang convertible. The tires squealed, and the car lurched to a halt behind a grimy dump truck. "Two feet to spare. No sweat."

Pastor Henke whipped out his handkerchief and mopped his forehead. "No sweat indeed. You may say 'no sweat' when you're driving your own vehicle and choose to tailgate a gargantuan mass of unforgiving steel." He caressed the dashboard. "It's all right, my dear little car. Healy is sorry he frightened the living daylights out of us."

The traffic light turned green, and the dump truck lumbered forward. Healy eased his foot onto the gas pedal and inched ahead. "Better?"

"Oh yes, much."

"You gotta remember, Pastor," Healy said, gliding onto the freeway on-ramp, "I haven't been behind the wheel of a car in over sixteen years. And as a teenager I didn't exactly drive like a grandma."

"Defensive driving is a virtue, my boy." The pastor cast Healy a scathing look. "And it's the *only* way you'll ever be allowed to drive my car again."

"Sorry, Pastor. I really do appreciate your helping me practice for my test." Healy flipped the turn signal, then checked both mirrors and glanced over his shoulder before changing lanes. "How was that?"

"Excellent. And a respectable distance between you and the car ahead. Let's keep it that way."

Over the next several miles Healy relaxed into his driving, finally giving up the urge to floor the gas pedal and see what the sweet little red sports car could do. He couldn't understand Pastor Henke's complaints, however. On more than one occasion he'd witnessed the pastor peel out of the driveway or church parking lot. He'd even been in the passenger seat numerous times when the old guy sat at a traffic light and gunned the engine in a taunting challenge to the driver in the other lane. Guess the pastor still cherished his fantasies of youth and speed.

Sounding more at ease, Pastor Henke said, "Have I told you the latest in the Marsha Sanderson saga? Take the next exit, by the way."

"I heard something about her and a friend being picked up at the Wal-Mart last weekend." Healy eased onto the exit ramp and turned right at the stoplight, passing an electronics store and some restaurants.

The pastor clicked his tongue. "Honestly, that child's mendacious nature is going to be the ruin of her."

"Pastor, how many times do I have to tell you? Your twenty-dollar words are wasted on my two-bit ears. Speak English, okay?"

"Sorry, my boy." He sighed. "I mean, as long as the Sandersons let Marsha get away with her lies, she will never straighten out. Once again, she has gotten another of her gullible friends in trouble."

"Seems to be a habit with her." They drove in silence past apartments, churches, and several housing subdivisions. Healy slowed as he approached a four-way stop. "Straight ahead?"

"Yes, then left at the next intersection. You're doing very well, Healy. My toes have finally uncurled."

Healy gave a low whistle and patted the steering wheel. "This little baby purrs like a kitten."

"She may purr for you all she likes. But remember, she only growls for me."

On the Interstate again, heading toward Aileen, the pastor continued his story about Marsha Sanderson's latest run-in with the law. "Naturally, our dear Marsha is out on bail while her friend Jackie sits in juvenile hall. However, there is a small break in the case," he added slowly, "someone who actually overheard the girls plotting the crime and witnessed their attempted escape."

"Oh yeah?"

"Yes." A pause. "Valerie."

The car swerved. Angry horns sounded to their right.

"Healy!"

"I got it, I got it." Healy's fingers bit into the steering wheel.

"My fault," the pastor murmured. They both sucked in sharp breaths. "I knew it would take you by surprise."

When they turned onto the quiet country road to Aileen, the calming scenery of shady oaks, farmland, and livestock grazing in the stubbly fields helped restore Healy's equilibrium. "How. . .how is Valerie involved?"

As the pastor talked, all Healy could think about was that Valerie had actually made it outside her home, successfully negotiating a trip to a busy department store. He almost burst with joy at the news of her accomplishment. *O Lord, thank You.*

Healy parked in the pastor's driveway and handed him the keys. "Thanks again for the driving practice. Next time I could use some pointers on parallel parking."

A pained look crossed Pastor Henke's face. He gulped. "I. . .suppose so."

Entering the kitchen, Pastor Henke said, "I'm afraid I don't have much time for preparing a meal this evening. I have an appointment to meet with Jackie and her parents tonight." He turned to Healy. "You're welcome to come along, if you haven't too much homework."

Healy smiled. "I'd like that." He still basked in the glow of his success with Tina Maxwell. If God could somehow use him to help young people stay on the right path and avoid life-altering mistakes like his, he wouldn't pass up an opportunity.

sixteen

A pale pink dawn filtered through the lacy curtains as Valerie reached for the creamy white journal. She'd filled several pages since beginning her therapy with Dr. Miller, and rereading her latest entries, she gave thanks to God. What a joy to discover that the underlying tones of sorrow and grief gradually faded before an ever-increasing sense of hope.

Now she must make one final entry. Uncapping her fountain pen, she turned to a fresh page.

My little one,

When I first started writing to you in these pages, my body and spirit were so broken that I was afraid I'd never find peace again. I still miss you and your daddy more than I can say. Your daddy would have loved and cherished you as I do your memory, and I thank God for the blessed assurance that you and Daddy are together in heaven now.

Child of my heart, it has been a long journey, but you would be so proud of your mommy. The old terrors are finally letting go. It all started when Healy Ferguson came into my life, and even though it was hard to face the truth about Healy's past, I am humbled daily by how dearly your daddy loved him as a friend.

I love him, too, deeply and inexpressibly. When we met, we both had so much growing and healing to do, but I believe this is also part of God's plan. Maybe we needed to find each other for the healing to begin.

So, my precious one, it's time for me to say a last good-bye to you—although you will always be a part of me. My love for you is forever sealed within these pages, but now I must look toward the future, which I pray will include Healy.

My greatest regret is knowing I may never be able to give Healy the family he deserves. I pray the doctors were wrong and that someday you may yet have a little brother or sister—not to take your place but to continue the legacy of love I so wanted to share with you.

I miss you, my darling, my sweet little baby. May God and His holy angels watch over your spirit and keep you ever in His presence.

> *Love always,*
> *Mommy*

Tears streamed down Valerie's cheeks as she closed the book. Tenderly she wrapped it in the pastel green mono-grammed baby blanket she had saved all these years. As she bent to tuck the precious bundle away in the bottom drawer of her dresser, a shaft of sunlight touched her left hand and set her engagement diamond ablaze. She sank onto the edge of the bed, her eyes brimming with fresh tears.

"Oh, Tom, I need to say good-bye to you, too, my love." She slipped her rings from her finger and held them to the light, gazing at them deeply, longingly, one last time. "Oh, my darling, I will always love you, but I know you would want me to be happy again. Please give me your blessing."

She removed another white box from the dresser drawer, this one containing her wedding album and mementos from that special day. Folded neatly atop the album lay the lace-trimmed white handkerchief her mother had given her to carry with her bouquet. She placed her rings within the folds and pressed the handkerchief to her lips for a parting kiss before closing it away with the other treasures.

Filled with new peace, she dried her eyes before going downstairs. She found Connor and Annie at breakfast. She poured herself a glass of orange juice and carried it to the table. "Where's Ellen?"

"Mommy's throwing up again." Annie seized her milk glass with both hands and took a big gulp. She swiped at a drip on her chin before scooping up a spoonful of multicolored O-shaped cereal.

The sound of running water in the downstairs bathroom preceded Ellen's ashen-faced appearance in the kitchen. "I thought this morning-sickness thing would have ended weeks ago. Must be another girl."

"That's an old wives' tale." Connor laid his paper aside and sipped his coffee. "Have you talked to your OB/GYN about why you're still throwing up so often?"

"I have an appointment this afternoon—" Slapping a hand over her mouth, Ellen raced toward the bathroom.

Connor stared after his wife, his brows drawn together. "She wasn't sick this long with Annie."

Valerie paused before filling a bowl with shredded wheat. "She seems to be feeling good otherwise. I remember even at five months I still felt nauseated sometimes. . . ." Her voice trailed off and she sighed. "Would you like me to go check on her?"

"Give her a minute. She prefers not to have an audience."

"I understand." Toying with her spoon, she stared into her bowl.

Connor touched her arm. "Are you sure *you're* okay? You look a little sad this morning."

"Not in a bad way. Just came to another crossroads, that's all." Two, actually, but she would savor those tender moments awhile longer before explaining to her brother.

Ellen returned, a wet washcloth pressed to her neck.

"Did you throw up again, Mommy?" Annie asked.

"Darling daughter,"—Ellen gulped and jammed a hand to her stomach—"you and your father will not use those words in my presence again." She heated water in the microwave and dunked a raspberry teabag in the steaming mug, then retrieved the box of saltines from the pantry. "So what's on everybody's agenda for today?"

"The usual office appointments, then a rhinoplasty later this afternoon." Connor adjusted his tie. "Should be routine."

Valerie finished a soggy mouthful of shredded wheat. "Annie and I are going to work on her reading skills after breakfast, and then Pastor Henke is taking me to my counseling appointment."

"And I'm going to look at storybooks in the waiting room." Annie lifted her cereal bowl and drained the last dribble of milk.

Ellen planted a kiss on Annie's head. "Great, you can read me one of your stories when I come home." She glanced at the clock. "I need to get a move on, or I'll be late picking up Healy for class."

Connor went to the cupboard and got his wife a travel mug for her tea. Walking her to the door, he enveloped her in a hug. "Hope you feel better, honey. Be sure to talk to your doctor about this morning-sickness thing—"

"Please, not another word." Ellen planted three quick kisses on her husband's lips and grabbed her purse. "Have a good day, everyone." The back door banged shut behind her.

After Connor left, Valerie helped Annie sound out words in a picture book and then finished getting ready for her appointment with Dr. Miller. On the drive over, Pastor Henke brought Valerie up to date concerning the latest prayer needs at church.

"And, of course, keep the Sanderson family on the list. I still pray for a miracle with Marsha."

"So do I." Valerie smoothed her khaki slacks, then stared at her folded hands. "Ellen told me Healy has been going with you to visit Tina and Jackie."

The pastor fairly beamed. "He is quite amazing with those troubled young ladies. They both seemed to trust him readily."

"I'm not surprised." She gazed out the window, only half listening while the pastor chatted on about Tina's and Jackie's spiritual and moral progress. A stab of remorse pierced her heart, and she silently apologized to the Lord for her indifference toward the delinquent teens. The person she really wanted news about was Healy.

Following her appointment, Pastor Henke took her and Annie to lunch at a small, colorfully decorated Mexican restaurant on Aileen's town square.

The waiter seated them at a corner table under a pink piñata in the shape of a pig. "I can't remember the last time I ate out," Valerie said before opening her menu. At least the restaurant wasn't busy yet. "Warn me if I get something stuck between my teeth, okay?"

Pastor Henke chuckled as he studied the menu. "The enchiladas *al carbon* are excellent here. Annie, what interests you, my dear?"

The curly-haired child seized a handful of tortilla chips. "Corny dog and french fries."

"A truly authentic Mexican dish. Good choice." Pastor Henke winked at Valerie.

The waiter took their order and returned shortly with their meal. Dabbing taco juice off her chin, Valerie noticed two men in business suits enter the restaurant. Recalling the church directory photo, she identified the taller man as Harold Sanderson, Marsha's father. She tapped Pastor Henke's ankle with the toe of her shoe.

He caught her eye and casually glanced over his shoulder. "Oh dear."

Mr. Sanderson sauntered over and offered his hand. "Pastor, good to see you. And Mrs. Bishop, isn't it? I understand you're still suffering from your, er, emotional distress. How are you doing these days?"

An icy shiver went up her spine. "Very well, thank you."

"Mind if I sit down?" Without waiting for a reply, the tall, beefy man pulled out the empty chair across from Annie. He inclined his head toward his athletically trim and equally well-dressed companion, now seated with his back to them at a table near the window. "That's our family attorney, Jason Albright. He's in the process of preparing a defense for Marsha and, of course, would be very interested to interview your psychiatrist, Mrs. Bishop."

Valerie cringed. "My doctor is a licensed Christian therapist, not a psychiatrist. And I'm sure she would be happy to answer any of your attorney's questions. Although I can't imagine how she could help Marsha's case."

The swarthy man cast Valerie an oily smile. "I've read that post-traumatic stress disorder can make people delusional, hear voices, confuse fantasy with reality."

Pastor Henke removed his glasses and glared at Mr. Sanderson. "Harold, your remarks are highly indecorous and patently uncalled for. Perhaps you should excuse yourself and stop insulting my friend and *your* fellow parishioner."

"Yes, well, we all know Mrs. Bishop hasn't been attending church services since she moved to Aileen." Sanderson returned the pastor's direct gaze. "And perhaps you should remember where a high percentage of Zion's financial support comes from. In addition, you might consider rethinking your associations, Pastor. First a mental patient—now I hear you've taken a convicted murderer into your home."

Valerie's mind burned with fiery retorts, but she couldn't find her voice.

"You should spend less time protecting your own reputation and more time reading your Bible," Pastor Henke countered. "Our Lord Jesus Himself welcomed all kinds of 'sinners' into His company."

Even as her own agitation heightened, Valerie sensed Annie's growing distress. The little girl drew her knees under her and leaned across the plate containing her half-eaten corny dog and ketchup-smeared fries. "You're a mean man and I want you to go away *right now*." She punctuated the last words with a pointed finger and accidentally tipped Pastor

Henke's glass of iced tea into Mr. Sanderson's lap.

"Why you—" The startled man bolted to his feet, expletives exploding from his mouth.

Sputtering, Pastor Henke grabbed for the overturned glass. An observant busboy rushed over with a dishpan and cloths. He swept the scattered ice cubes into the pan and mopped up the table and floor in front of the fuming Mr. Sanderson, then made a rapid departure.

Valerie wanted to shove her hands over Annie's tender ears, but the child continued her own tirade against the "mean, mean man."

"Annie," Valerie pleaded, "please sit down and be quiet, okay?" With trembling hands, she grabbed a napkin to dab at the ketchup now staining the pink-and-green appliquéd watermelon on the front of Annie's new shorts set.

"This is an outrage," Jason Albright shouted, joining the mêlée. "Believe me, Mrs. Bishop, I'll remember this when we go to court. You are certainly an unfit caregiver if you can't even prevent a small child from such an impudent display."

"Unfit—how dare—" Valerie's hammering heart threatened to explode right out of her chest. She thought she would surely expire right here in Don Reynaldo's Mexican Restaurant, face down in her Acapulco Special.

"Enough!" Pastor Henke bellowed. "Gentlemen—and I use that term loosely—you will please leave this establishment at once, or I guarantee you will both be hearing from *my* attorney."

With departing glowers, Sanderson and Albright stormed out of the restaurant.

Valerie fought to keep from collapsing into a quivering mass of raw nerves. Pastor Henke came to her side and wrapped a protective arm around her. "It's all right now, it's all right. They're gone."

"Oh, wow, I handled that well." Gasping, she took a shaky sip of water. At least Annie had settled down and now calmly polished off her corny dog.

"I'd say you handled the situation very well indeed, all things considered." The pastor pulled up the chair Harold Sanderson had so brusquely vacated and sat down close to Valerie. "Take a moment to pull yourself together, and I'll drive you home as soon as you're ready."

At the sound of someone clearing his throat, Valerie glanced up in dread. A thin, dark-complexioned man with a moustache stood next to Pastor Henke's chair. "Pastor, please accept my apologies. I was tied up on a phone call when the wait staff informed me two men were harassing you. Can I assist you in some way? Should I call the police?"

"That won't be necessary, Ray. This is a problem we'll have to entrust to the Lord."

"If the need should arise, both the waiter and busboy witnessed everything. They agree the other men started the altercation."

"Thank them for me. I'll call if their help is needed." The pastor turned to Valerie. "Are you ready to go home, my dear?"

She nodded and attempted to stand on quivering legs. Her breathing had yet to return to normal, and tears threatened.

Pastor Henke reached for his wallet, but the man stopped him. "Today your meal is compliments of Don Reynaldo's. I only hope you will return another day, when perhaps you can enjoy a more pleasurable dining experience."

❧

Hours later, in the seclusion of her darkened sitting room, Valerie finally calmed down enough to relate to Connor and Ellen what had transpired at the restaurant.

Ellen's fists knotted. "I always knew there was something I didn't like about Harold Sanderson. What a creep."

Connor sat on the floor, his back resting against Ellen's knees. "Three cheers for our Annie-girl, though. Wish I could have seen Harold's face when that iced tea landed in his lap."

Valerie curled her legs under her and hugged a throw pillow.

"Mr. Sanderson really scared me, and I don't just mean the panic attack. I seriously believe he intends to use my emotional illness to discredit me as a witness against Marsha."

Ellen shook her head. "The man will go to any lengths to keep his daughter out of trouble so *his* reputation won't be soiled. What is wrong with people like that? And how did he ever become a member of Zion Community Church?"

"His wife, Donna, is a good Christian woman," Connor stated. "However, I don't think she has the intestinal fortitude to stand up to him."

"How do you know so much about her?" Ellen asked.

"I, uh. . .I have to plead doctor-patient confidentiality."

"Aha, so Donna Sanderson is a patient of yours." Ellen narrowed her eyes. "Interesting. Tummy tuck? Nose job?"

Valerie mentally tuned out the conversation as she laid her head on the arm of the loveseat. *Father, I know You are fully capable of protecting me and bringing good out of this for all of us. Grant me a huge dose of Your courage, because I have a feeling I'm going to need it. . .and very soon.*

⁂

Healy headed to the campus cafeteria to grab something for supper and do a little studying before his evening carpentry class. It had not been one of his better days. He got an important date wrong on his history quiz, and math problems he had solved easily last week now baffled him. When he tried to wade through a chapter of his business textbook, his eyes blurred. An uneasy feeling plagued him, but he couldn't identify the source.

A church friend picked him up later and drove him home to an empty house. He found a note on the kitchen counter from Pastor Henke saying he would be late because of a committee meeting. Tired as he was, Healy propped himself up in bed to make a last-ditch attempt at his reading assignment. His eyelids grew heavy and his mind soon went numb from trying to absorb endless facts and figures.

Around ten forty-five, the pastor returned, tapping lightly on Healy's door. "Still up, are you?" the white-haired man asked with a yawn.

"Not for long. Can't seem to concentrate."

"I've had one of those days, too." Pastor Henke sighed, a faraway look in his eyes. "I'll tell you about it in the morning. For now, let's both try to get some sleep. Good night, my boy."

" 'Night, Pastor." Finally giving up on his studies, Healy turned off the lamp and settled into bed.

Sleep eluded him. For hours he tossed and turned, kicked covers off, punched his pillow, got up for a glass of water, adjusted the speed of the ceiling fan. Nothing seemed to help.

"Lord, You must be keeping me awake for a reason. What is it?"

Valerie. Pray for Valerie.

His throat tightened as an image of her delicate face formed in his mind. He fought the urge to wake the pastor, but by now it was almost two o'clock a.m., and he could hear the elderly man snoring loudly even through two closed doors.

"Okay, God, You know what's wrong, and You know what Valerie needs. Be with her and protect her from whatever danger she faces. Calm her with Your holy peace."

As he murmured his "amen," a measure of God's peace settled over him as well, and his restlessness finally ebbed.

seventeen

"Val?" Ellen's voice sounded muffled through the closed bedroom door. "It's almost nine. Honey, are you getting up?"

Valerie rolled away and pulled the thin cotton blanket up around her chin. Since her encounter with Harold Sanderson at the restaurant, every day had been a struggle. One moment she felt strong and confident. In the next the phone would ring or a car horn would sound, and she'd be trembling from head to toe.

A persistent knock sounded from the hallway. This time she heard Connor's voice. "Valerie, you promised you'd go to church with us. Don't chicken out on me, sis. You can do this."

Yes, she'd promised. . .in a weak moment. Connor had the bright idea that if Valerie showed up in church, it would undermine Harold Sanderson's ability to cast doubt upon her reliability as a witness.

And Marsha's hearing was set for Tuesday morning.

Valerie's stomach lurched. She lunged to the bathroom and hung over the commode seat, succumbing to dry heaves.

The outer door opened and Ellen slipped in. She dampened a washcloth and pressed it into Valerie's shaking hand. "Looks like you're doing worse than I am this morning. Today's the first day I *haven't* thrown up."

Valerie laid the cool cloth against her cheeks and glimpsed her pallid face in the mirror. "Maybe Harold Sanderson is right. I'm such a bundle of nerves, why would anyone believe anything I had to say?"

"You don't believe that for a minute." Ellen angled a stern gaze at Valerie's reflection. "You have the power to finally make the Sandersons face the truth about Marsha. If you back out, who knows what kind of trouble that kid will get herself into by the time she's twenty?"

"Oh, Ellen, why does it have to be me?" Then she thought of Healy. Suppose an adult had taken a firm stand with him and his sister, rebuking Healy for his temper, insisting Bethy abandon dangerous relationships? Would a man's life have been saved, sparing Healy sixteen years of regret and inner torment?

"Okay. I know you're right." She leaned against the bathroom sink and drew in a shuddering breath. "I need to shower and wash my hair. Do I have time?"

Ellen drew her into a hug. "We'll make time."

The congregation had just risen for the opening hymn when Valerie and the Paige family entered. Connor found seats on the back pew, placing Valerie on the end in case she felt the need for a quick departure. For a dizzying moment, her thoughts flashed back to the last time she'd worshipped at Zion—when she and Tom visited Connor and Ellen the Easter before Tom's death. She closed her eyes and let the memories wash over her. Blessed relief filled her when she felt more gratitude than sorrow in remembering. Tom had once been her whole life, her very reason for living. But he was gone, and nothing would ever bring him back. She must look toward the future now, whatever God had in store for her.

She opened her hymnal as the organ strains of the familiar tune evoked timorous sounds from her vocal cords. *O God, it's been too long. Thank You for bringing me back.* She focused on the words and music of "What a Friend We Have in Jesus," and soon found herself singing with joyous enthusiasm.

੨*

As Healy attempted the tenor line of his favorite hymn, he glanced around hoping for a glimpse of the Paige family. Valerie had been heavily on his mind and in his prayers for days now, even more so after Pastor Henke told him about her unnerving experience at Don Reynaldo's. Another family occupied the Paiges' usual pew today, he discovered with chagrin. He prayed it didn't mean Valerie's condition had worsened to the point that they didn't want to leave her home alone.

From a few rows behind him, a strangely familiar voice caught his ear, a voice he couldn't recall hearing at Zion before, and yet. . .

He casually turned his head, scanning the faces at the rear of the church. His gaze settled on the petite, fair-haired woman standing near the aisle in the very last pew.

Valerie.

The words of the hymn froze in his throat. His heart leaped. It was all he could do to resist the urge to shove aside the people next to him, charge down the aisle, and sweep her into his arms.

Her gray eyes met his. She wiggled her fingers in a shy greeting as a bittersweet smile curled her lips. He smiled back, then ducked his head and swiveled to face front again.

When the service ended an hour later, he had not the remotest guess as to what scripture lessons had been read, the subject of Pastor Henke's sermon, or even who had been mentioned in the congregational prayers. He thought he would explode before the others in his pew finished their after-worship hellos and chats and finally made room for him to exit.

ॐ

"Carol and Dave O'Grady, I'd like you to meet my sister, Valerie," Connor said, introducing her for what seemed to Valerie like the hundredth time.

"How do you do? Nice to finally meet you in person." She recognized many names. A few people she remembered meeting when she and Tom had visited. She'd read about some of the other families in the church newsletter or heard Connor, Ellen, or Pastor Henke speak of them. Several people she knew from her prayer-chain phone calls, or personally from evening Bible studies hosted at the Paige home. Others were part of the congregational care team that visited her on occasion. All expressed delight to see her out and about at last.

When space cleared around her, she tried not to be too obvious as she stood on tiptoe to look for Healy. *Oh, please, Lord, don't let him have left without speaking to me.*

Just when she thought she glimpsed him beyond some bobbing heads, another face filled her vision.

"Mrs. Bishop."

Her blood ran cold, but she bravely lifted her chin. "Good morning, Mr. Sanderson." She felt Connor's arm slip around her waist, giving her the courage to cast the towering man a confident smile. "Sir, you look surprised to see me."

"I—" He cleared his throat. "I'm so glad to see you're well enough to worship with us this morning. But I wouldn't want you to become so overwrought from these little outings that you are unable to appear in court this Tuesday."

She hoped he couldn't hear her throbbing pulse. "How kind of you to be concerned. However, I wouldn't dream of missing the opportunity to do my civic—and Christian—duty."

A plump, mousy woman appeared at his side, with a bored-looking Marsha lingering a few steps behind. "Harold, dear," said the woman, "we should be going."

Something prodded Valerie to reach for the woman's hand. "Mrs. Sanderson, I'm so glad to meet you." She ignored Harold's icy glare. "I've been praying for Marsha. I know you only want the best for her, but sometimes what's best for our children is that we *don't* protect them from the consequences of their mistakes."

"Yes, I. . .I know." The woman glanced toward her husband. "It's been hard—"

"Donna," Sanderson snapped, seizing her wrist, "let's go."

The woman cast Valerie an apologetic grimace as her hulking husband dragged her toward the exit. Marching behind her parents in a self-righteous huff, Marsha suddenly whirled around and narrowed her gaze at Valerie. "People like you, you just don't get it with your holier-than-thou attitudes. Stop sticking your nose where it doesn't belong."

The teen's words stirred an angry passion in Valerie. She followed them outside into the glaring noonday sun.

"Mr. and Mrs. Sanderson." She caught them at the edge of the sizzling parking lot.

The man spun around. "Careful, ma'am, or you really will work yourself into a state."

"You tell her, Dad."

"Harold, please—"

Valerie took a long, steadying breath and spoke in measured tones. "Sir, there is absolutely nothing you can do to hurt me more than I have already been hurt. My wounds go deeper than you can possibly imagine. And why you would waste your time attempting to rattle me enough that I would appear incompetent before a judge is beyond me."

She paused, searching his face, searching for the right words. Her gaze drifted briefly to Marsha. "You have a lovely daughter who is going to grow up not knowing right from wrong. You're teaching Marsha that no matter how badly she messes up, Daddy's going to fix it. But she'll be an adult soon, and Daddy won't always be able to cover for her mistakes. Then what?"

"Dad, are you going to let her talk—"

"Marsha, be quiet." Donna Sanderson tugged on her husband's arm, looking up at him with a tear-streaked face. "Mrs. Bishop is right, Harold. It's long past time someone held Marsha accountable."

Marsha screwed up her face. "Mom—"

"First your brothers and sister, now you—this has gone on too long, and it has to stop."

Valerie became aware of Pastor Henke beside her.

"Harold," he said, "are you listening? How much trouble does Marsha have to get herself into before you finally tell her enough is enough?"

The man faltered. "She's just a kid, Pastor. Kids make mistakes. That's part of growing up."

"It doesn't have to be." The low, insistent voice at Valerie's left commanded everyone's attention. Healy stepped forward. "You want to hear about mistakes, Mr. Sanderson? How about if somewhere down the line Marsha finally does something bad enough to get her sent to prison? How will you feel then? Let me tell you, it's no walk in the park."

Sanderson lifted his chin. "How dare you—"

"How dare I what?" Healy leaned into his tirade. "How dare I tell you about real life, about what could happen when a kid takes a wrong turn and gets away with it? About how one 'free ride' gives you the guts to take the next chance, and the next?"

He moved to stand directly in front of Marsha, his determined gaze penetrating her defiant one. "Young lady, if you had any clue what real jail time is like, you wouldn't be looking so cocky right now. You'd be on your knees before the judge on Tuesday, begging for mercy."

Relentlessly he bombarded her with the gruesome details of his life in prison: the embarrassing lack of privacy, fights—or worse—with other prisoners, daily harangues from arrogant guards, not to mention the sometimes grueling, often disgusting manual labor.

The girl's lower lip trembled. She took a small step backward and lowered her eyes. "I. . .I didn't do anything. It was them. Tina and Jackie."

Valerie found her voice once more. "No, Marsha. It was you. And it's time you admitted it."

ஐ

Healy watched tiredly as the Sandersons got into their silver Lexus and drove away. He could only hope he'd gotten through.

And Valerie—she was amazing. She and the Paiges stood in the shade of a cherry tree a few feet away. Valerie hugged herself and sucked in huge gulps of air. Her brother and sister-in-law patted her back and spoke encouragement while their tow-headed daughter scooped up a handful of dried grass clippings and tried to entice a skittery blackbird. At least Ellen had kept little Annie out of the fray.

"Here, looks like you need this." Pastor Henke handed him a folded white handkerchief.

Healy took it gratefully and drew it across his damp forehead, then wiped his perspiring palms. The heat seemed even more oppressive today, or was it merely his nervous tension?

He shook his head. "When I saw Valerie in the back pew, I was flying higher than a kite. And then. . ." He lifted his hands in a helpless gesture.

"And then the Sandersons happened." Pastor Henke released a tired groan. "It certainly appeared Harold and Donna—even Marsha—were moved by what you and Valerie said. Let's pray for a miracle, shall we?"

Healy nodded toward the family under the cherry tree. "My miracle is standing right over there."

"Then don't you think it's about time you told her so?"

Maybe it was. The past few weeks had brought Healy a long way toward the maturity and sense of personal completeness he'd been striving for. Returning to school had brought a measure of confidence, and a contact he had made through the vocational department promised steady part-time work with a reputable building contractor.

And maybe. . .someday. . .he'd have the experience and resources to start up his own construction business.

Hope and a future, the years of the locust restored. *Lord, thank You.*

An even fuller sense of satisfaction swelled because of the time he spent with Pastor Henke at the juvenile detention center. Last week the pastor had introduced him to a chaplain heading up a new troubled teens ministry, and the man had encouraged Healy to join him.

Yes, if God could finally bring some good out of those wretched prison years, Healy would cooperate 100 percent.

The pastor nudged him and gestured toward the Paiges. "Er, Healy my boy, you're about to miss your opportunity."

Healy looked up to see Connor unlocking the Paige family minivan. Panic spurred him into action. No way was the woman of his dreams getting away from him today. He sprinted toward the parking lot. "Valerie, wait."

eighteen

At the sound of her name, Valerie's heart climbed into her throat. Healy jogged toward her, his eyes filled with single-minded purpose. How many times had she prayed for this moment? One foot on the running board, her fist wrapped around the handgrip, she stared at the approaching figure and dared to hope.

She recalled her first glimpse of Healy in church this morning, sensing something different about him even then. His dishwater-blond hair, though still brushing his collar in the shaggy style she found so endearing, had been neatly trimmed. He no longer wore homeless-barrel hand-me-downs or Tom's slightly too large shirts and jeans. Today he looked casually handsome in pressed khakis and a trim-fitting blue plaid polo shirt.

But he also carried an air about him that went much deeper than surface appearances. She'd never seen him looking so relaxed and self-assured. No one meeting him for the first time today would ever suspect he had been a troubled youth, much less believe he'd served time in prison. When he spoke his mind to the Sandersons, his natural eloquence filled her with awe.

In truth, the only thing about him that seemed unchanged was the telltale scar disfiguring his left forearm. Yet even the scar spoke of his godly character, especially after Pastor Henke had told her the story behind it one day as he drove her to an appointment with Dr. Miller.

Panting, Healy staggered to a halt within arm's reach of her, and she realized her own breath had quickened. He opened his mouth, but no words came out. He jammed his hands into his pockets and backed off a few steps. That purposeful air of only minutes before had vanished, replaced by a cloud of uncertainty.

"Healy, hi!" Not yet buckled in, Annie jumped up from the seat and poked her head between Valerie and the door frame.

"Hey, munchkin." A hesitant smile briefly eased the tension lines in Healy's face.

The little girl grinned flirtatiously. "Did you come over to kiss Aunt Val?"

"Annie Maureen Paige!" Ellen twisted around and gaped at her daughter, but the twinkle in her eye betrayed her delight.

Valerie's cheeks flamed. She lowered her gaze as Ellen reached around to guide the little girl back inside the van. With Connor's help, Ellen buckled Annie into her safety seat.

Then, lowering her window, Ellen spoke to Healy. "Actually, we're all dying to know. *Did* you run all the way over here to kiss Valerie?"

Valerie gasped. She noted with chagrin that Healy's embarrassment matched her own. And yet he displayed a grin a mile wide.

"Truth be told, ma'am, I sure would like to." He cast Valerie a sidelong glance. "That is, if the lady consents."

She inhaled a deep, shaky breath. Of course she wanted to kiss him, desperately! She fingered a loose strand of hair falling across her shoulder. "Um. . .maybe we should go somewhere and talk first."

Pastor Henke appeared beside Healy. "I, er, didn't mean to eavesdrop, but. . ." He jangled a set of keys. "Healy, my boy, the Mustang is yours if you'd like to borrow it for the afternoon. I'm sure Connor and Ellen will be happy to drop me off at home."

Valerie eyed Healy with a puzzled smile. "You're driving now?"

"Passed my test a couple of days ago." Turning, he caught the keys as the pastor tossed them over. "Thanks, Pastor."

"Treat her with respect, my boy," Pastor Henke cautioned.

"The car, that is. I know you'll do right by Valerie."

"Yes, sir." Healy gave a mock salute.

Pastor Henke winked at Valerie, then gently bumped her aside and climbed in beside Annie.

Slack-mouthed, Valerie found herself standing on the hot pavement alone with Healy. She kicked at a loose pebble with the toe of her beige leather pump. "Looks like I'm stranded. Care to give a girl a lift?"

"My chariot awaits." Healy escorted her to the pastor's shiny red convertible.

Once both their seatbelts were fastened, he turned to her and grinned, one eyebrow lifted provocatively. He revved the engine a few times before steering the car out of the parking space in a slick maneuver rivaling James Bond.

Valerie smiled in mute admiration and gripped the armrest. She finally released her pent-up breath when he slowed three blocks later and turned in at the Sonic Drive-In. Pulling into a space next to one of the menu boards, he lowered the windows and shut off the engine. A warm, zesty breeze swept through the car, ruffling their hair.

"It's not fancy," he said with an apologetic half smile, "but it's within my budget. Hope it'll pass for Sunday dinner for you this once."

After all Valerie had been through this morning, sitting in the privacy of the car at a drive-in sounded just fine—in spite of the fact that even in October it remained ninety degrees in the shade, and the humidity must be close to 100 percent today. "Works for me. What do you recommend?" She undid her butterfly clip and wound all her hair off her damp neck before replacing it.

Healy ordered burgers, tater tots, and cherry limeades, then added into the speaker, "Make that order to go, please." Glancing at Valerie, he said, "Thought we could have a picnic. There's a small lake nearby, with a neat spot the pastor showed me. It's shady and breezy. . .a nice, quiet place where we could talk."

Valerie nodded. The delay would give her that much more time to calm her roiling emotions and regain some perspective about this incredible new man sitting beside her.

❧

Healy hoped he appeared calmer than he felt. Under his new plaid shirt from JCPenney's—bought with money he'd earned replacing kitchen faucets for one of Zion's parishioners—his heart roared louder than the Mustang's supercharged V8 engine.

Maybe he was rushing things. Valerie had an awful lot to cope with, what with her scheduled court appearance Tuesday and all the hassle the Sandersons had been giving her. But to look at Valerie now, so poised and serene, not a worry line in sight to mar that beautiful brow. . . *Oh, dear Jesus, thank You for the miracle of healing You are performing in her life. And let me be worthy, if it's Your will, to share my life with her.*

The server brought their order. Healy passed the bags over to Valerie, and she balanced them on the floorboard next to her feet. Leaving the Sonic, Healy suggested they put the top down on the convertible and forego air conditioning in favor of the brisk breeze. Conversation proved impossible over the wind noise, but Healy didn't mind. He could use the time to settle his nerves and frame his words. There was so much he needed to say to her, and he had no idea where to begin.

He parked near a secluded picnic area overlooking the sun-dappled lake. A sharp gust of wind whipped around the car as he helped Valerie out. "Hold on to your skirt. The breeze is really picking up."

As they settled opposite each other on benches at a sheltered picnic table, a sudden gust toppled the bag containing their burgers. Valerie snagged a loose napkin. "Maybe we'll get lucky and a cool front will come through."

"That would suit me just fine." Healy peeled back the foil wrapper on his burger. "Even better if it brought some rain. The lake looks even lower than the last time I was here."

When at last Healy had deposited all but their limeade cups in a nearby trash receptacle, he climbed onto the bench next to Valerie so that both of them looked out toward the wind-stirred whitecaps dancing across the lake.

"Thank you for coming with me." He reached tentatively for her hand, sighing inwardly when she intertwined her fingers with his.

She glanced wryly at him and took a sip of her drink. "Face it, neither of us stood a chance with Ellen, Annie, and Pastor Henke all playing matchmaker."

A fuzzy sensation tickled his insides. "Matchmakers, huh? How do you feel about that?"

"Well, I. . .I sort of liked it." Her voice softened to nearly a whisper. "How about you?"

Healy almost couldn't make out her words over a deep rumbling in the distance. Probably a truck on the highway. Or maybe a jet, he reflected as a shadow passed over the lake.

When the sound subsided, he answered, "I liked it, too." He stared at their entwined hands. "I don't want to put any pressure on you, I mean, with all you're facing right now, but. . ."

"But what?"

He looked up, and their gazes locked.

But I'm deeply, crazily in love with you, Valerie Bishop, and I can't spend another day without you. His chest pounded so violently that he couldn't catch a full enough breath to speak the words.

Her shimmering eyes became pleading. "Say what's on your heart, Healy. Don't be afraid. I'm not. Not anymore."

His gaze drifted to the gently curving bow of her lips. White heat shot through him. "Maybe if I"—he leaned closer—"could just kiss you. . ."

Those sensuous lips arched into an inviting smile. "I thought you'd never get around to it," she said huskily, and laced her arms around his neck.

Healy thought he would drown in the ocean of love filling

those gorgeous gray eyes. He drew her close, pressing his lips against hers, tasting their warm sweetness until tears coursed down his cheeks.

"I love you, I love you," he murmured against her hair, holding her ever more tightly. "These last few weeks—I missed you so much. I can't even imagine my life without you in it. Somehow. . .some way. . .I want to prove myself worthy of your love in return."

"You don't have to prove anything to me, Healy Ferguson." Her words fell against his ear in warm, breathy wisps. "You are worthy. I've known it—and I have loved you—almost from the day we first met."

He pulled back, searching her face. "You have?"

She nodded.

A sudden thunderous *crack* startled them both, and Valerie buried herself in his arms. Her heart beat like a fluttering bird against his chest.

Only then did he notice how dark the day had grown. A mass of thick, ominous clouds swept in from the northwest. On the metal roof above them came another sound, almost unrecognized after the long, dry summer—heavy, clattering raindrops. He looked out at the dry ground and watched huge drops splatter in the dust. Ever-expanding rings formed as rain pelted the surface of the lake.

Autumn rains.

It felt like a sign from heaven confirming the promises of the scripture Healy had clung to for so long. *Thank You, Lord.*

The next gust of wind carried a chill, and the fat, spattering drops abruptly became a downpour. Valerie lifted her head and burst out laughing. "Rain! Healy, it's finally raining!"

nineteen

Healy's momentary elation erupted in a panicked cry. "Oh no, the car!"

He raced to the car, leaped over the door, and scrambled into the already drenched driver's seat. He stabbed the keys into the ignition, then pressed the switch to raise the top. "Come on, *come on!*" He thought it would never reach the up position and finally lock into place.

He looked up to see Valerie dancing around puddles and shielding her head with both hands. She fell into the passenger seat and slammed the door. Her rain-soaked hair hung limply around her shoulders. Mud speckled her dainty beige pumps.

He grinned at her. "You look like a drowned rat."

She pushed a wet curl off his forehead, sending a shiver down his spine. "You look. . .incredible."

He took her hand and simply held it, gazing at her while the rain thundered against the roof. In a matter of seconds, their warm bodies and breath had the windows completely fogged. His conscience urged him to turn the car around and get them home at once, before the love in Valerie's eyes and the seclusion of their damp but cozy cocoon destroyed what little resistance he had left.

❧

Valerie gazed through the rain-spattered side window and sent up a prayer of thanks that Healy's willpower proved stronger than hers. Having experienced the full breadth and depth of married love, she longed to share such closeness again. . .as Healy's wife. She believed with all her being that God had brought them together.

But she also knew that they must wait. Their love was still so young, and they had much to talk about, so many issues yet to deal with.

Including Marsha Sanderson's appearance in juvenile court on Tuesday.

The rain had let up by the time they reached the Paige house. Valerie ran inside long enough to grab several towels, then helped Healy dry the car interior as much as possible.

"Do you think anything's ruined?" she asked as Healy wiped water drops off the dashboard.

"Sure hope not." He frowned. "But I doubt Pastor Henke will ever let me near his car again."

"We were both taken by surprise. You got the top up as quickly as you could." She drew the towel around the stick shift and center console.

Healy knelt on the driver's seat and tugged at a strand of her wet hair that had come loose from the butterfly clip. "That storm isn't the only thing to take me by surprise today."

Her pulse quickened. "Me neither."

Healy helped her carry the damp towels to the laundry room and start the washing machine. Standing on the back porch, he sighed and shoved his hands into his pockets before bending to kiss her lightly on the lips.

Recognizing the wisdom of his posture, she locked her arms behind her back. "Call me?"

"Count on it."

When she turned from closing the door, she found herself staring into Connor and Ellen's eager faces. Suppressing a smile, she brushed past them and headed toward the stairs. "I'm desperate for a long, hot bath," she announced without pausing. "I am soaked to the skin."

Let them wonder.

❧

Healy checked the thermometer outside Pastor Henke's kitchen window—a pleasant fifty-eight degrees. Fall had finally arrived! He slipped a crisp khaki windbreaker over his white dress shirt and navy print tie. He wanted to look his best when he met Valerie at the courthouse for Marsha's hearing.

"Ready, Healy?" Pastor Henke reached for his car keys on the kitchen counter. "I shall drive, naturally." He'd been none too happy to learn that his precious automobile had suffered even a few moments under Sunday's unexpected torrent.

Half an hour later, they gathered with Valerie and the Paiges in the corridor outside the courtroom of the Honorable Judith K. Houser. Healy had been in this same courtroom for Tina Maxwell's hearing, and he knew the judge to be fair-minded and frank.

Good, just the kind of judge to deal with Marsha Sanderson.

And, he hoped, the kind of judge who would make sure the Sandersons' attorney didn't emotionally abuse Valerie.

He edged close to the woman he loved and took her hand. "How are you doing?"

"Nervous."

He detected a slight tremor in her hand and gripped it more firmly.

"Val, they're calling everyone inside." Connor nodded toward the bailiff standing in the open courtroom doors. He planted a quick kiss on her cheek. "We'll be waiting for you right here, and praying like crazy."

Valerie inhaled deeply. "I'll need all the prayers I can get."

With Healy holding her hand, they followed the Sanderson entourage into the small, wood-paneled courtroom. Jason Albright shot them a scathing glance. Healy fired back his own threatening glare as he drew a protective arm around Valerie's shoulder.

At least the Sandersons themselves no longer displayed the same animosity toward Valerie. Healy hoped Marsha's red-rimmed eyes signified true remorse, not a dramatic performance intended to impress the judge. If only she would show even a hint of the willingness to turn her life around that both

Tina and Jackie had demonstrated.

Lost in prayer, he paid little attention to the court proceedings until the juvenile prosecuting attorney called Valerie to the stand. His senses sharpened, and his gaze riveted on the slender blond woman as she strode to the witness chair. Healy could tell by the set of her mouth and the way she repeatedly smoothed the fabric of her dark green dress that every moment was a battle for control.

The prosecutor's questions were simple and straightforward, allowing Valerie to relate the Wal-Mart incident in her own words. After a few minutes, the tight lines around her mouth relaxed, and she spoke as if she and the attorney were the only ones in the room. At least Jason Albright had the decency to keep his mouth shut. After all, how could he object to the truth?

"Thank you, Mrs. Bishop. No further questions at this time." The prosecutor returned to his chair.

Judge Houser finished jotting some notes on a legal pad and looked toward the defense table. "Mr. Albright?"

"Yes, Your Honor, thank you." The slick lawyer rose and buttoned his suit coat. He ambled toward the witness stand and presented his arrogant profile to those seated in the courtroom. "Mrs. Bishop, how are you today?"

Healy read phoniness in every aspect of the man's demeanor. He stiffened.

"I'm fine, thank you, Mr. Albright." Valerie folded her hands and smiled serenely back.

"No hallucinations today, no voices, no panic attacks—"

"Objection," snapped the prosecutor. Healy wrestled back the urge to leap across the railing and nail Albright on the chin.

Judge Houser removed her glasses and glared at the Sandersons' attorney. "Objection sustained. Mr. Albright, you will please confine your questions to the matter at hand."

"Your Honor, my question cuts to the heart of this witness's credibility. The defense intends to prove that Mrs. Bishop's mental health issues—"

"Must I remind you, Mr. Albright, that Mrs. Bishop is not on trial here today. The court is fully aware of Mrs. Bishop's 'mental health issues,' as you choose to call them, and you are surely aware of Dr. Karen Miller's deposition in which she describes the causes, treatment, and, I reiterate, *excellent* prognosis for Mrs. Bishop's recovery from post-traumatic stress disorder."

The judge flipped through a file on her desk. "So unless you have some new evidence that would convince the court otherwise, I find no reason to excuse Mrs. Bishop's testimony on the grounds you are claiming."

For once, Jason Albright look flustered. "Er, in that case, Your Honor, the defense requests a brief recess."

"Very well. Ten minutes."

"But, Your Honor—"

With a tired sigh, Judge Houser folded her arms atop the desk. "Mr. Albright, all the time in the world isn't going to change the facts. Either you are ready to proceed with your client's defense, or you are not."

"I object, Your Honor."

The judge pinched the bridge of her nose. "To what, Mr. Albright?"

Jason Albright lifted his chin. "To the fact that Your Honor has obviously already decided this case before hearing the defense arguments."

"*If* that is true, then you are the only one to blame. You seem to have forgotten your job, sir, which is to present *credible* evidence on your client's behalf. Now, do you want that ten-minute recess or not?"

Albright swallowed. "Yes, Your Honor."

Healy winked at Valerie and caught the almost imperceptible relaxation in her shoulders.

The judge turned to Valerie with a look of mutual understanding. "Mrs. Bishop, you're excused for the time being. Thank you for your patience."

❧

In the corridor, Valerie tucked her arms under Healy's jacket and sagged against his warm chest. "Is it over?" she asked tiredly. "I mean, my part?"

Connor patted her shoulder. "From what little we overheard, it sounded like the judge did a good job of putting Albright in his place. I can't imagine he'd dare try anything else."

Ellen smoothed Valerie's hair. "You did great, honey. How are you feeling?"

Valerie and Healy shared a knowing look. "I should get an Academy Award."

"You've got my vote." Healy touched her cheek. "How are you doing, babe, I mean really?"

She liked the sound of that, *babe*. "Actually, I'm doing great. I feel. . .*empowered*. I feel triumphant. Like I've just survived the Boston Marathon. More than survived—*conquered*."

All the while she was on the stand, she had mentally repeated a scripture verse from Isaiah: *"You will keep in perfect peace him whose mind is steadfast, because he trusts in you."*

Perfect peace. Was it possible, after so many years, that she had found it at last?

The bailiff's strident announcement brought an abrupt end to the ten-minute recess. Judge Houser swept in, her black robes billowing, and Healy and Valerie took their seats.

The judge peered at Jason Albright. "Shall we continue?"

Albright rose and cleared his throat "Your Honor, Marsha Sanderson has asked to speak on her own behalf."

Valerie grasped Healy's arm. Perhaps what they'd all been praying for would finally happen.

"Very well." The judge gestured Marsha to the witness stand. "Young lady, what is it you would like to say?"

Marsha lowered her eyes, her hands clasping and unclasping. "I–I'm really sorry for what I did."

"Before you say anything further, dear. . ." Judge Houser

fixed Jason Albright with her steely gaze. "Mr. Albright, have you discussed with your client the possible implications of what I believe she is trying to tell this court?"

"Yes, Your Honor, I have." Albright's jaw muscles flexed. "Marsha Sanderson and her parents have made this decision against my advice. Miss Sanderson wishes now to throw herself upon the mercy of the court and accept whatever disciplinary actions your honor deems appropriate."

"I see." The judge cast her patient gaze upon Marsha. "All right, dear, in that case I'd like you to explain exactly what it is you are sorry for."

More hand wringing and a desperate sidelong glance toward her parents. "I'm sorry for. . .for talking my friends into shoplifting and then lying about it so I wouldn't get blamed."

Thank You, Father! Valerie gave Healy's arm another squeeze, and he patted her hand, nodding almost imperceptibly. If not for the solemnity of Judge Houser's courtroom, both of them would surely have leaped and shouted for joy.

twenty

It had taken a full week for Valerie to come down off her post-trial high. She savored the heady feeling of wholeness and inner peace, hers at last by God's grace. And yet, despite the long years of grief and fear, she knew in her heart that God had never abandoned her, never stopped being in control of her healing.

The greatest blessing of all was God's wonderful gift of Healy. They grew closer and more in love every day, spending as much time together as his class schedule and part-time work would allow—and no longer within the confines of the Paige house. Yet those few short hours they shared together each day didn't seem nearly enough, and Valerie could barely control her urgency for things to change.

In the meantime, she'd been contemplating how to solve another problem. Though they'd taken Pastor Henke's car to the detail shop for a thorough cleaning and waxing, it appeared he had only grudgingly forgiven them for leaving his precious red Mustang unprotected during the downpour.

In a last-ditch attempt to win him over, Valerie invited him for tea and fresh-baked brownies—from his favorite bakery in town, not homemade, she quickly informed him. The next afternoon, while Annie watched a favorite movie on the den TV, they nibbled brownies and chatted in the Paige kitchen.

"My dear Valerie, homemade or not, these are delicious." The pastor dabbed crumbs off his chin with a paper napkin. "Not on my diet, of course, but a delightful treat."

She topped off his cup of Earl Gray. "I've been meaning to ask you about Marsha. What's the latest news?"

"She's none too happy about serving time in detention,"

the pastor replied, "but I think it has finally put the fear of God into her, and I hope I mean that literally. As you know, Healy's troubled teen ministry is now involved with her case, and it appears her shell is beginning to crack."

He blew across the surface of his tea and took a sip. "And the Sandersons are now attending my biblical parenting class. Donna had to coerce Harold with untold threats to get him to their first session, but he has made an astounding turnaround in a very short time, praise God."

"That's wonderful, a real miracle." Valerie smiled coyly and rested her chin on her interwoven fingers. "Certainly such encouraging news should more than make up for any remaining hard feelings over the completely unintentional blunder of your two very favorite parishioners."

The white-haired man eyed her suspiciously. "First you ply me with brownies, then you play upon my good humor. Since I am already quite willing to forgive you and Healy for your negligence, I am afraid to ask where all this munificence is leading."

She traced a finger around the rim of her teacup. "I need to retake my driver's test, too, before I can get a new license. Your little red car is so cool, and I was hoping. . ."

"Oh no. No, no, *no*!" He lifted his hands. "I was fool enough to entrust my precious automobile to Healy, and look how he repaid me. And on top of everything else, the ungrateful lout is planning to move out and leave me to fend for myself once again."

Valerie's heart lifted at the reminder of Healy's return to the garage apartment next Saturday. Connor had already discussed additional remodeling projects with him, a top priority being the new baby's nursery. And transportation to school and work was no longer a problem since Healy had arranged to purchase a reliable used car from a church member. In every aspect, he grew more independent and self-possessed with each passing day.

The pastor laid a hand on Valerie's arm. "You know my petulance is all a sham. I could not be happier for any two people in the world than I am for you and Healy."

She leaned over to kiss his round, ruddy cheek. "After all, you're the one who introduced us."

He wiggled his bushy white eyebrows. "So. . .should I anticipate a wedding in the near future?"

"As much as I want that, it's way too soon. We still have issues to work through." Her throat tightened. "Pastor, I haven't told him everything yet about the night Tom died."

His brows drew together. "Oh, my dear, do you think it will matter to him, honestly?"

"But he loves Annie so. And look how great he is with the kids at the detention center. He'd make a wonderful father. He deserves children of his own."

The pastor grasped both her hands and held them firmly. "But he is in love with *you*."

"I know." A tear slipped down her cheek. *But I wanted to give him so much more.*

Later, when Healy stopped by between his after-school construction job and a teen ministry board meeting, she grabbed a sweater and took him out to the wicker rockers on the back porch. Cheery clusters of yellow and orange chrysanthemums filled the porch-rail planter boxes, and the whole earth smelled moist and alive again.

"You look like you have something on your mind." Healy pulled his chair closer, his forehead wrinkled in concern.

In the gathering darkness she absently massaged the empty spot on her ring finger and struggled for words. "Healy, the night Tom died. . . I never told you the whole story."

She could feel him tense. His mouth grew tight. "It's okay. You don't have to."

"Yes, it's important that I do." She set her chair to rocking, hoping the rhythmic motion would soothe her, but it only served as a poignant symbol of a joy she might never know, the joy of rocking her own child.

"When it happened," she began, her throat constricting, "I was five months pregnant. My baby died that night, too."

Healy exhaled sharply. "I know, babe. I'm so sorry."

"You know about my recurring back pain." She forced herself to continue before courage failed her. "One of the men pushed me backward, and I fell across one of those metal picket fences they put around trees in the sidewalk. That's what caused me to lose the baby. And the internal injuries I suffered. . ." She swallowed a sob. "Healy, there's a good chance I may never be able to have more children."

He knelt at her feet and enveloped her in his strong arms while she gave in to her grief all over again. When her tears subsided, he pressed her hands between his own. "My precious Valerie," he said, his eyes filled with tenderness, "if you thought telling me this would change my feelings for you. . ."

She sucked in her breath, both anxious and terrified to hear his next words.

Healy's voice grew husky. "At this moment my feelings for you are deeper and stronger than they've ever been. You are the bravest, most loving woman I have ever known or ever hope to know."

"Oh, Healy, I'm sorry, I'm so sorry." She pressed her face against the collar of his soft flannel shirt and twined her fingers through his hair.

"You have nothing to be sorry for." He drew her once again into his sheltering embrace. Then his body stiffened, and his tone became tentative as he added, "Unless this is your way of saying you want me out of your life."

She pushed him to arm's length but kept her hands locked around his neck. "That's the last thing I'd ever say to you, Healy Ferguson." Her chest ached, her heart pulsed. "Healy, if you'll have me, I want to spend the rest of my life showing you how much I love you. I want to be your wife."

Healy recoiled as if she had punched him in the belly. He

sputtered, fumbled for words, raked a trembling hand through his hair. "Hey, I know I missed out on a lot while I was in the slammer, but I thought the guy still did the proposing. Anyway," he added with a chuckle and a downward glance, "I'm the one on my knees here."

Valerie looked at him with puzzled amusement. "In case you haven't noticed, this is the twenty-first century. Not that I'd exactly call myself a women's libber, but I have learned how to ask for what I want." She tapped her toe with mock impatience. "Now, is that a yes, or a no?"

With a crooked smile he lifted her left hand and caressed her fingers. Abruptly he stopped and held her hand toward the amber glow of the porch light. His brows knitted. "You're not wearing Tom's rings. I hadn't noticed before. When did you take them off?"

With a tender sigh, she thought back to the day she'd said her final good-byes to Tom and the baby she would never hold in her arms. "A few weeks ago, when I realized how desperately I wanted to spend the rest of my life with you."

"But are you absolutely sure? You and Tom, you had so much—"

"Tom was my first love. Yes, what we had was amazing and wonderful, and it can never be replaced." A tear slipped down her cheek. "But the love I feel for you, though different, is equally strong. And I think I can love you better for having loved Tom. . .and for knowing how much Tom loved us both."

Speechless, his own depth of passion shining in his eyes, Healy drew her ring finger to his lips and kissed it. She caressed his face with the palm of her hand before brushing away a streak of dampness from his cheek. She cast him an expectant glance. "You still haven't said yes to my proposal."

"Yes," he said in an explosion of laughter and tears. "Yes, yes, *yes!*"

epilogue

"All rise."

Valerie reached for Healy's hand as they stood with their attorney to await the entrance of the Honorable Judith K. Houser. How appropriate they should find themselves in Judge Houser's courtroom again after all these years, and for such a significant occasion. The statuesque judge, who now presided over family court, settled into the leather chair behind the bench.

"My, my," the judge began when the rustle of shuffling feet and chairs had ceased, "this is quite a family I see before me, Mr. and Mrs. Ferguson." Slipping on her reading glasses, she perused the contents of a thick file folder. "Four happy children, all thriving, I see."

A lump rose in Valerie's throat as she glanced over her shoulder. On the long bench behind them, sandwiched between Connor and Ellen on one end and fourteen-year-old Annie and her ten-year-old brother, Thomas, on the other, sat four fidgeting children, each as different from the others as night and day.

Jenny, age seven, wore her chin-length black hair in a smooth bob. Five-year-old Kim rubbed sleep out of her dark, almond-shaped eyes, while her coffee-complected younger brother, Andrew, age four, bounced the toes of his polished shoes off the railing in front of him.

Tucked under Annie's protective arm sat three-year-old Bethany, her blond curls rivaling Annie's. Soft green eyes danced in her round, flat face. She grinned at Valerie. "Mommy, I love you."

"I know, sweetie. Mommy loves you, too."

"Let's be quiet now." Annie gave Bethany a quick kiss on the top of her head.

Judge Houser lowered her reading glasses. "Mr. and Mrs. Ferguson, your petition to adopt little Michael appears to be in good order."

Sighing inwardly, Valerie gazed with tenderness at the seven-month-old baby sleeping in the infant seat on the table in front of her. Healy reached his arm around her. He looked handsomer than ever in his cocoa brown suit and paisley tie, especially with the distinguished flecks of gray at his temples.

Continuing, the judge folded her hands. "Before I grant this adoption, however, I have a few things to say. Mr. Ferguson." She fixed intense brown eyes on Healy. "The court is, of course, fully cognizant of your background and the challenges you have had to overcome to reach this place in life."

Healy bit his lip and nodded. Under the table, Valerie patted his knee.

"I must say," the judge continued, "your diligent efforts to establish yourself as a model citizen are well documented. I well recall your frequent appearances in my juvenile courtroom on behalf of teens in trouble. I have also read with great pleasure the innumerable letters of commendation written by everyone from your pastor, to the warden and chaplain where you served your sentence, to your former college instructors and employers."

Judge Houser slipped on her glasses to consult her notes before continuing. "This latest home-study report describes you as an exceptional father and a conscientious provider for your family. I see that you are the successful owner of your own construction business, the cornerstone of a vibrant ministry for troubled youth, an elder of your church. . ." She paused and caught her breath. "Sir, I applaud you for a life well lived."

Healy cleared his throat. "Thank you, Your Honor."

"I would also like to commend both you and your wife for opening your home and hearts to special-needs children, those dear ones who are so often overlooked by today's society. I see that your church has assisted you in adopting orphans from China and South America"—she nodded toward Kim and Jenny—"and also that you are parents to a biracial son and a daughter with Down's syndrome. Admirable indeed."

Little Michael squirmed and whimpered. Valerie reached for his pacifier and patted his tummy until he quieted.

"And now," Judge Houser continued, "you are petitioning to adopt a little boy suffering from fetal alcohol syndrome. With any other couple I would seriously question your preparedness for such an undertaking. But I have only to look into the faces of your other four children to know that you have not only the necessary patience and tenacity but an endless supply of love."

The judge lifted her gavel. The firm *crack* echoed throughout the courtroom. "Petition granted. Congratulations, Michael Connor Ferguson. In my considered opinion, you are one of the luckiest little boys in the world."

A cry of joy erupted from Valerie's throat. She and Healy fell into each other's arms. Moments later their other children, along with Connor and his family, Pastor Henke, and Valerie and Connor's mother, pushed through the gate and encircled them with more hugs and tears.

"I think this calls for a prayer of thanksgiving," Healy said in a choked voice. One arm around Valerie, the other hovering protectively over baby Michael's infant seat, he bowed his head. "Gracious heavenly Father, again You have shown the power of Your promise. What a quiver full of children You have given me. Thank You for my precious wife, Valerie, and for the wonderful blessings these dear little ones have brought into our lives. Help us always to be the best parents we can be and to model Christ's love for them. In Jesus' holy name, amen."

"Amen indeed," Pastor Henke interjected. "'Be glad, O people of Zion'!"

A Letter To Our Readers

Dear Reader:
In order that we might better contribute to your reading enjoyment, we would appreciate your taking a few minutes to respond to the following questions. We welcome your comments and read each form and letter we receive. When completed, please return to the following:

Fiction Editor
Heartsong Presents
PO Box 719
Uhrichsville, Ohio 44683

1. Did you enjoy reading *Autumn Rains* by Myra Johnson?
   ❏ Very much! I would like to see more books by this author!
   ❏ Moderately. I would have enjoyed it more if

   _____

   _____

   _____

2. Are you a member of **Heartsong Presents**? ❏ Yes ❏ No
   If no, where did you purchase this book? _____

   _____

3. How would you rate, on a scale from 1 (poor) to 5 (superior), the cover design? _____

4. On a scale from 1 (poor) to 10 (superior), please rate the following elements.

   ____ Heroine   ____ Plot
   ____ Hero   ____ Inspirational theme
   ____ Setting   ____ Secondary characters

5. These characters were special because? _____

_____

_____

6. How has this book inspired your life? _____

_____

_____

7. What settings would you like to see covered in future
   Heartsong Presents books? _____

_____

_____

8. What are some inspirational themes you would like to see
   treated in future books? _____

_____

_____

9. Would you be interested in reading other **Heartsong
   Presents** titles? ❏ Yes ❏ No

10. Please check your age range:
    ❏ Under 18   ❏ 18-24
    ❏ 25-34   ❏ 35-45
    ❏ 46-55   ❏ Over 55

Name _____

Occupation _____

Address _____

City, State, Zip _____

E-mail _____

LOVE IS A
BATTLEFIELD

Take a walk in Shiloh
National Military Park
with battling park
rangers, Ace and Kristy,
as the park's history
proves that true love
really does exist.

Historical, paperback, 320 pages, 5¾" x 8"